Sherlock Holmes and The Sword of Osman

To Peter Jackson
with my best wishes!

Tim Symonds

Dec. 2018

Paperback: 978-1-78092-755-8
ePub: 978-1-78092-756-5
PDF: 978-1-78092-757-2

Published in the UK by MX Publishing
335 Princess Park Manor, Royal Drive, London, N11 3GX
www.mxpublishing.com
Cover by www.staunch.com

Tim Symonds in Gavdos (photo Lesley Abdela)

Tim Symonds was born in London. He grew up in Somerset, Dorset and the Channel Island of Guernsey. After several years in the Highlands of Kenya and along the Zambezi River and two years in Canada he emigrated to the United States. He studied at the University of California, Los Angeles, graduating Phi Beta Kappa in Political Science. He is a Fellow of the Royal Geographical Society.

Sherlock Holmes And The Sword of Osman was written in a converted oast house near Rudyard Kipling's old home, Bateman's, in the English county of East Sussex, and completed on Gavdos, a remote island in the Libyan Sea, off Crete.

Other detective novels by the author include
Sherlock Holmes And The Mystery of Einstein's Daughter,
Sherlock Holmes and The Case of the Bulgarian Codex, and
Sherlock Holmes and The Dead Boer at Scotney Castle.

To LJA

Contents

Chapter I   A Letter Arrives from Deepest Africa 9

Chapter II   We Meet The Mysterious Ornithologist ...19

Chapter III   We Prepare For Constantinople 37

Chapter IV   We Board HMS Dreadnought 53

Chapter V   We Meet The Khan Of Khans 71

Chapter VI   The Sword Of Osman 93

Chapter VII   We Meet The Chief Armourer's
Widow 107

Chapter VIII   We Engage In Smoke And Mirrors 123

Chapter IX   Holmes Makes An Unexpected
Deduction 135

Chapter X   We Pay Chiarezza Another Visit and Say
Goodbye To Our Dragoman 149

Chapter XI   A Most Surprising Letter Arrives From
Mycroft 175

Postscript 197

Notes From The Author 198

Acknowledgments 204

For six centuries until the last sultan was exiled in 1924 the Sword of Osman was a vital element in the ceremony enthroning each new ruler of the Ottoman Empire. The sword was named after Osman I, founder of the Ottoman Dynasty. Its possession conferred both temporal and spiritual power and declared the ruler 'lord of all and everything'.

Chapter I

A Letter Arrives from Deepest Africa

IT was the spring of 1906. Another warm, hazy Edwardian summer lay just over the horizon. Gone were the harsh winter months with seas of fog so thick a gondola would be of more use on London's streets than a carriage. In my pocket was a communication posted some six months earlier from the interior of the African Continent. It contained a stupendous invitation to come to the Congo to set up a medical hut among the Pygmies. It was signed by a P. J. Pretorius. I marvelled at the many pairs of feet and forked sticks which brought the letter from the depths of Ruanda to Mombassa in British East Africa and thence by Royal Mail to my consulting rooms in Marylebone. There had been a time in my boyhood when the map of the world was full of blank spaces. Now only the heart of Africa and the Amazon rainforest remained.

I left my premises for the calm of Regent's Park and found a bench looking out over the boating-lake. Gentlemen of leisure were taking their morning walk. I was gratified to note a few strollers carrying copies of *The Return of Sherlock*

Holmes, a selection of my cases first published in *The Strand Magazine* with original illustrations by Mr. Paget. Other visitors sat reading magazines on benches along the quiet pathways.

The dramatic invitation to the Congo had arrived at an opportune time. For the first time in decades I was free to control my own fate. My former comrade-in-arms Sherlock Holmes had announced his retirement three years earlier following the *débacle* of the Dead Boer at Scotney Castle, a taboo never mentioned. Europe's greatest private consulting detective had simply declared a wish to forego the 'interesting little problems' so plentifully presented by the political, financial, and trading capital of the world in favour of spending his remaining years tending bees on a remote farm in the Sussex countryside.

On his retirement Holmes explicitly forbade me to prepare the case-notes on the Dead Boer for publication. Expelled from a world of murder, swamp adders, daring burglaries and ancient rituals, I abandoned the pen for a blunter instrument, the scalpel. My days were now spent at my surgery removing infected tonsils or treating Lord E. for the pox for the umpteenth time. I sorely missed Holmes's high-pitched blasts on his cab whistle followed by an exhilarating leap into a nimble hansom while he shouted 'Cabbie, Paddington Railway Station—the slope entrance. Half a sovereign for yourself if you can catch the 9.15'. There had only been one adventure together in the last twelve months, our journey to the Balkans to investigate the mysterious fate of Lieserl, the half-Serbian daughter of a young physicist by the name of Albert Einstein.

Pretorius's invitation revived an old craving of mine to wander in distant and dangerous lands. I yearned to trek through the great forests where the upper waters of the Congo River rise, so vividly described in Conrad's wild story *Heart of Darkness*. 'The Congo is a mighty big river ... resembling an immense snake uncoiled, with its head in the sea, its body at rest curving afar over a vast country, and its tail lost in the depths of the land'.

'Its tail lost in the depths of the land,' I repeated in wonder.

Rider Haggard's *King Solomon's Mines* was another fabulous tale that fired my dreams of Africa: 'Yes,' answered Sir Henry, 'it is far. But there is no journey upon earth that a man may not make if he sets his heart to it. There is nothing that he cannot do, there are no mountains he may not climb, there are no deserts he may not cross...'

My letter accepting Pretorius's invitation completed, I went to bed that night in high anticipation. Disease, like crime, is a code waiting to be broken. I would set about my work on the Equator in exactly the way Holmes approached the circumstances, life history and character of suspects in a crime.

The next several days would be filled with frenetic activity. A visit to Thomas Cook and Sons on Oxford Street to check on shipping schedules, followed by the Army & Navy stores for clothing and yards of carbolised bandages, cotton wadding and medicines. I would have to suffer an uncomfortable hour or two at the dentist to ensure my teeth were in the best of health.

Four weeks later, however, matters took an abrupt turn.

Rather than the Suez Canal, Swahili and the forest giraffe I was to find myself starting on a thousand details of life at the heart of the Ottoman Empire.

* * *

The case of the Sword of Osman started on the very day I left the surgery to walk the two miles or so to St. Mary Axe to reserve my boat-ticket for Africa. I was well into my stride and approaching Madame Tussaud's when a messenger waving a telegram drew up alongside on a bicycle, like a coracle berthing at a pier. My locum had given the lad directions of my intended route together with a description of my attire. I commended his initiative and sent him on his way with a thrupenny bit and a push.

The telegram was from Holmes. It read, 'Dear Watson, if you can throw physic to the dogs for an hour or two I would appreciate meeting at the stone cross at Charing Cross railway station tomorrow noon. I have an assignation with a bird-lover at the Stork & Ostrich House in the Regents Park which has excited my curiosity. Yrs. S.H.'

Truly delighted as I was at hearing from Holmes the message left me puzzling. There was nothing to explain why such a humble invitation would excite Holmes's or anyone else's curiosity. Perhaps long sterile weeks lay behind him—he hoped against hope there was a fitting object for his special powers. I went back over the words carefully. His curiosity had been excited by an assignation at the Stork & Ostrich House in the Gardens of the Zoological Society of London. My former comrade was a world expert on classical ciphers. Was the telegram in code?

The idea Holmes would agree to an assignation at the Stork & Ostrich House in Regent's Park was absurd. Did 'Stork & Ostrich House' stand for something more sinister— key-words warning me that what immediately preceded or followed was not to be taken at face value? Was there to be a final showdown with the evil Colonel Sebastian Moran in full view of Marabou storks?

I marched on to the shipping agents to order a commodious cabin for the journey to East Africa. I would get them to wangle me a guest room at the Mombassa Club on arrival.

* * *

Exactly on time Holmes emerged from the railway station. I had not seen him for almost a year. I regarded my friend as an Old Testament son of Anak, thrusting up through the schists and gneiss of ordinary mankind. A boxer and fencer, light in weight, powerful and enduring. The face was still clear-cut, the complexion ruddier than before, but he looked rather bent as he walked towards me, as though repeated exposure to the South Downs winters was doing him no good. The well-worn footpaths he followed, used for centuries by farmers, tradesmen and locals to get from one hamlet to another were wide open to the blasts of cold air sweeping up from the Seven Sisters. I grasped his hand warmly, saying, 'I trust you are well?'

'Thank you, Doctor,' Holmes replied. 'This horse has pulled a heavy load a long way but I'm well looked after.'

He gave me a questing glance.

'And your medical practice?'

'As absorbing as ever.'

13

'Ah yes,' he responded, his grey eyes twinkling. 'I always liked that about you. You blush when you lie.'

'Unlike you,' I reposted.

I realised how pleased I was to see my old friend again.

'I note you still smoke the Arcadia mixture of your bachelor days!' he observed. 'There's no mistaking that fluffy ash upon your coat.'

'Is it true we are to visit the Zoological Gardens?' I asked.

'It is.'

'The Stork & Ostrich House?'

'The very spot,' he assented, grinning at my perplexed look.

'I should ask after your bees,' I resumed. 'How are the blighters?'

'The past winter's ceaseless wind and rain kept them—and me—penned indoors longer than usual,' came the reply.

He stopped to light a cigarette in his familiar nonchalant manner and resumed, '...then one day, a sudden warmth brought out the blossom of the cherry plum. A gap in the rain—and there they were, above the hive, like a puff of smoke.'

I walked him towards a Double Brougham, listening politely to this unusually poetic disquisition. I could scarcely wait to impart my own vastly more exciting news but my comrade went on updating me with life on the Sussex Downs, even how he would label the jars of honey pilfered from the unwilling beasts.

By the time he finished, the cab had carried us almost to the top of Portland Place. Eagerly I told Holmes of my intention to remove myself from a world of fashionable ailments in which my principal advice to well-to-do women was to throw away their swan bill corsets. I would soon be on the High Seas—the Bay of Biscay, the Mediterranean Sea, in convoy through the Suez Canal and the Great and Small Bitter Lakes to the Indian Ocean, steaming southwards to one of the hottest and most humid places in the world. While the cab clattered on its final stretch to Regent's Park I passed the Pretorius letter to Holmes.

He read the pages carefully without a change of expression.

'Well, Watson,' he remarked with no trace of a smile, 'you wish to replace civilized days at the Gatwick Races and the Junior United Services Club with swamps and deadly scourges? I imagine a clearing in the Congo is one of the most absolutely infernal places of residence for a pair of solitary white men. Nevertheless, my dear friend, if you are intent on going, you must impress the natives. I shall insist that Thomas Cook—at my expense—supply you with at least a score of mules, half a dozen reception tents, kitchens and water-carriers.'

This was followed by a further silence. I prompted, 'And your visit to the Zoological gardens?'

I was handed a letter on the headed notepaper of the Zoological Society dated the prior week. It began, 'Dear Mr. Holmes, I beg you to forgive the temerity in writing to you without first a formal introduction. I do so *à titre privé* as Secretary of the Gardens of the Zoological Society, at the request of a member of the Society who wishes to meet you on a certain matter. He plans to publish a work of ornithology on seasonal visitors' birdsong—the cuckoo, meadow pipits, spotted flycatcher, redstart, turtle dove and so on. He proposes to enquire into the movements of a *rara avis* reported on the South Downs. If you can be persuaded to return to London for an hour or two may I suggest a meeting at the Stork & Ostrich House here at the Zoological Gardens in Regent's Park this coming Friday, at 2pm? A member of my staff will await you at the North Entrance at the quarter to. We would be greatly honoured if you would accept.'

The letter ended, 'I am, with great truth and respect, sir, Your Excellency's most obedient, humble servant, Peter Chalmers Mitchell FRS DSc LLD.'

I passed the letter back, saying 'Well, Holmes, in all our years at Baker Street I don't believe I heard you comment on the various squawks and screeches of our avian friends except the once, in Devon, to speculate whether the mallard quacks in regional dialects. Since you entered the life of a hermit you know how often I've tried to get you away from your bee-boxes and the solitude of the Downs for a day or two.'

Jokingly I added, 'What of the interruption to your next opus, *The Meadow-flower in Mesolithic Honey Cultures?*'

His reply was patient but veering to the condescension of old.

'Come, come, my dear chap, naturally I accepted. I accepted at once. Did you ever come across anything as ludicrous? Ornithological spies have infiltrated my few acres and heard birdsong scarcely known to mankind, like coming across a Mayan temple on the South Downs or a new element for the Periodic Table. It's entirely preposterous. I suggest it's a case which may prove to have something in it or may prove to have nothing, but which at the very least presents *outré* features as dear to you as they are to me.'

The prospect of an investigation had energised Holmes.

He continued, 'Consider the words "Shall we say this coming Friday at 2pm?". Note how he sets a time without offering an alternative.'

'Setting a time to meet hardly seems *outré*,' I retorted. 'Not offering an alternative choice says what?'

'That this bird chappie must have serious obligations which he can break for only a short while. The nameless member of the Zoological Society must be a man of consequence, of *especial* consequence, tied in some unknown way to the Capital. Why else invite me to meet in Regent's Park— why not meet on my own territory, in the South Downs? Take cognizance of the hour. He suggests 2pm. If we are to be entertained by bird-song, why the afternoon? That's the very time of day when birds do *not* sing. The warmer air fails to carry the sound as far or as loud as cooler morning air.'

Holmes turned his familiar deep-set eyes on me.

'And why the Stork & Ostrich House—are such creatures famed for their contralto singing voices? My curiosity has been piqued. I want to know what lies behind this request.'

'My dear Holmes,' I protested. 'I see you still can't take anything in this world at face value! Does everything have to come under the scrutiny of a jaundiced eye and a ten-power magnifying glass? This request may be exactly what it says. After all, Sussex faces out on a vast Continent, and birds…'

An impatient wave stopped me in full flight.

'Watson, old fellow, it may not turn out to have the excitement of the case of the Bulgarian Codex but something is afoot. I ask you, why does the writer of this letter point us to the Zoo's North Entrance? Look at this!'

He thrust a square of paper at me headed 'Visitors' Plan of the Zoological Society's Gardens'.

'What of it, Holmes?' I queried. 'What am I to look at?'

'Visitors are urged to follow the dotted line. Where do the dots commence?'

'At the Main Entrance,' I replied, perplexed. 'Where else would they start?'

'Exactly so!' Holmes exclaimed triumphantly. 'It says "Passengers should be dropped from their carriages at the Main Entrance". I am invited to meet at the North Entrance, even though it's much further from the Stork & Ostrich House.'

I frowned, still unconvinced.

'What of the North Entrance?' I questioned.

'It can only mean our visitor wishes to remain incognito. The sighting of a *rara avis* on my bee-farm indeed. It's equally likely our visitor will prove to be a rare bird too. That particular entrance leads us to the Regent's Canal which we cross by a bridge and straight away take the tunnel under the Outer Circle. Surely that can only be to avoid photographers who spend their days lying in wait at the Main Entrance for visitors of high importance.

'Incidentally,' he added, 'the suggestion of an opus on the meadow-flower in Mesolithic honey cultures may be a notable example of your pawky wit but one well worth my consideration.'

Chapter II

We Meet The Mysterious Ornithologist

WE paid off the carriage at the North Entrance to the Zoo. The pair of dappled greys clopped away. A polite young man greeted us. He led us past the Winter Cranes House and the Kangaroo Paddock and across the canal bridge. The tunnel took us under the Outer Circle. A light wind gusted between the cages as we approached the Stork & Ostrich House, where our guide left us.

Inside the building a zoo keeper was addressing a group of children. He singled out a stork.

'The Abdim's Stork is also known as the White-bellied Stork,' he told them. 'The name commemorates the Turkish Governor of Wadi Halfa in Sudan, Bey El-Arnaut Abdim. Note the grey legs and bill and red knees and feet. At 29 inches it's the smallest species of stork, and weighs just over 2lbs.'

'Just like that boy Howie,' one of the girls whispered loudly. The other girls tittered.

The guide continued.

'The White-bellied Stork is distributed in open habitats

from Ethiopia south to South Africa. It prefers locusts, caterpillars and other large insects although the bird will also eat small reptiles, amphibians, mice, crabs and eggs. By contrast with another stork, the Shoebill, this species is welcomed and protected by local African belief as a harbinger of rain and good luck. In the breeding season it develops red facial skin in front of the eye and blue skin near the bill.'

Another schoolgirl whispered 'Just like Jimmy Webster' and again the gaggle tittered.

My impatience was growing. It was my intention to spend just the half-hour and then to leave Holmes and the mysterious visitor to discuss matters ornithological while I wended my way to the Army & Navy stores to purchase my tropical outfit and a new camera. For the latter I had arranged for a demonstration of the Lizars 1/4 Plate Challenge Model E.

My plan to get to the Army & Navy stores before closing-time was in jeopardy. I was consulting my watch ostentatiously for Holmes's benefit when a man in his mid-forties entered the Stork & Ostrich House. He wore a grey mackintosh buttoned to the neck, grey gloves and a fawn-coloured fedora with a light blue band around the crown. I judged the hat had been made by Teresio Borsalini. The front of the brim was snapped down as though to ward off the sharper rays of the sun.

'Gentlemen,' he said, removing a glove and offering a hand, 'my apologies for keeping you waiting.'

He gazed at Holmes.

'We have not met before, sir, but I am conversant with

your appearance from the society pages. I am very grateful to you for coming such a long way. And to you too, Dr. Watson.'

'For my part,' I returned, 'I am now on my way. I merely came…'

Before I could mention my destination and reason for visiting the Army & Navy Stores, Holmes intervened.

'Don't dream of going, Watson. I very much prefer having a witness, if only as a check to my memory.'

He turned to our visitor with an odd stare.

'I understand you are compiling a work of ornithology, sir, hence your interest in a certain bird spotted on my bee-farm.'

'Exactly so,' our visitor nodded, with an evasive smile. 'My interest in birds is long standing.'

'The title of your book?' I asked politely.

'The publisher suggests *The Charm of Birds*, though I ask you to be patient. It may not make an appearance in the book-shops for some years yet.'

Holmes gestured towards the inmates in the cages.

'Storks and ostriches are not especially mellifluous song-sters. And on names, sir, you clearly intend to maintain your advantage over…'

As he spoke these words, my comrade gave a start of recognition.

'Why, of course! Sir Edward! Shall we dispense with the pretence of the search for the wayward marsh tit. Could you explain precisely why you inveigled me here?'

I threw Holmes a startled look. Why was he calling our visitor 'Sir Edward'?

The man's response was immediate. He reached up to undo the top buttons of his coat. A black lounge jacket peeped through the open neck, followed by an edge of black waistcoat. The folds of a black cambric cravat were held together by a silver stick pin with a plain jet centre.

'Mr. Holmes, you must forgive the charade,' he replied. 'Yes, you are the *rara avis* I had in mind. I asked to meet here inside the Zoological Gardens because I adjudged the location the least likely for anyone from the newspapers to catch sight of us together and only half-an-hour by carriage from where I am myself caged. I shall come to the point at once. Mr. Holmes, you and Dr. Watson…' and here he offered me a courteous inclination of his head, '…could be pivotal in investigating a matter which could cause cataclysms right across Europe and raise great difficulties for our overseas Empire too.'

He halted, giving Holmes an enquiring, almost comical look. 'May I ask how you divined my identity?'

'My dear sir,' Holmes replied, 'you seem well-acquainted with my methods. I'm sure you can answer your own query.'

'I cannot. You made a deduction, but how?'

'The very palpable effort to cover something up,' came the breezy response. 'It was not so much the mackintosh itself but the fact it was buttoned up. We are experiencing remarkable warmth so early in summer. It was my supposition you might be determined to hide some particular fact or condition behind your outer garb which made me look for a clue elsewhere.'

'Elsewhere?' our confederate exclaimed, squinting down at his half-boots. 'This footwear doesn't seem exceptional for a stroll around the Zoological Gardens.'

'Not downwards, Sir Edward. Upwards,' Holmes responded, smiling. 'The first clue was revealed by the very hat you thought would help hide your identity.'

Overcome with curiosity I intervened, 'What of the fedora? It's a very fine…'

'Not so much the fedora, Watson.'

'Then?'

'The petersham band around the crown.'

Holmes motioned at the light blue ribbon.

'It's been placed hastily. See how it doesn't sit right. Also there's a slight difference in the nap of the crown resulting from an earlier presence, a tight band about two inches in width attached by those remaining black threads. Only the deepest mourning would call for such a wide crape band. Then when Sir Edward unbuttoned his coat it was confirmed the period of mourning has not yet ended.'

'Of course!' I burst out. 'Sir Edward *Grey*, the Foreign Secretary!'

'Precisely,' Holmes affirmed. 'Not wishing to be identified on his way here, almost certainly Sir Edward scrummaged around in the House of Commons and came across a boater belonging to a Cambridge graduate from which he filched the band, intending to replace it on the fedora with the black crape on his return to the House.'

I had failed to recognise the Foreign Secretary, so utterly out of context in the Zoological Society Gardens and buttoned to the hilt. I recollected a newsreel portraying Sir Edward along a stretch of river, catching trout on the dry-fly. Without apparent effort the line went out straight as an arrow, as light as thistledown, fisherman, line, rod, cast and fly all in unison. His face was regularly caricatured by Spy for *Vanity Fair* and pictured in the newspapers, especially so the previous February with the announcement of his bereavement. His wife Dorothy had been thrown from a carriage while driving near their Fallodon estate and died three days later.

'My deepest condolences for your loss, sir,' I said.

The next moment, as though feeling guilty at concealing the signs of mourning, Grey drew off a glove and exposed on the third finger a plain jet ring with a surround of hair set in crystal.

'A lock of her hair,' he explained, tapping the ring with a sad look. 'I carry everywhere a letter I'd half-written on the morning of the accident. I shall hand it to her when she and I are reunited in the Hereafter.'

'Sir,' I offered, 'the effect on your work, though it cannot be weighed or defined, must needs be very great.'

He looked at me appreciatively.

'As you would know personally, Dr. Watson. Your wife passed away at a similar age, I believe. I shared with Dorothy all my mind, all my happiness, all my pursuits. There are times when I get to my feet in the House of Commons and stare out at the faces of the Opposition, or sense scorn among those at my back or side on the Government benches... only quarter in jest I beg a kindly Providence to lose me my seat. I could retire from public life without reproach. Nevertheless I had to carry on. It was she who begged me to seek re-election to Parliament but I tell you, gentlemen, I'd far rather catch a three-pound trout on the Itchen than make a highly success-ful speech in the House.'

Sir Edward motioned towards a path.

'Perhaps we can retire to a quieter part of the Zoo.'

As we walked he went on gravely, 'I owe you a complete explanation. I presume I can speak in the utmost confidence?'

'Certainly you may!' I assured him energetically. 'Why, Holmes and I have kept confidences of the most sensitive nature—for example, when a certain member of one of the highest, noblest, most exalted families in England, His Grace...'

Holmes broke in swiftly.

'What my good friend Watson means is that you have our guarantee that nothing which passes between us...'

'...of course I have,' Grey broke in. 'This won't be the first matter of State brought to your attention involving the safety and wellbeing of nations. It's said you hold the honour of half the British peerage in your keeping and know that the other half has no honour to lose. I'm well apprised of the invaluable assistance you gave England in another matter in which the security of our country was compromised. Dr. Watson...' again he bowed slightly in my direction, '...titled the case *The Adventure of the Naval Treaty*. The matter to hand is of an importance at least the equal, and one might say the long-term consequences greater.'

'Sir Edward, you say this is a matter of State,' Holmes pressed. 'Why do you wish to engage my small talent rather than that of Scotland Yard or the hundreds of diplomats at your disposal?'

Sir Edward pointed to the North exit. 'I have a trap outside. If you'll follow me, there is something I'd like to show you.'

By now I was late for my appointment at the Army & Navy Stores but my curiosity was growing by the minute. We were with a man in whose palm lay every lever controlling the Empire's foreign policy. What in heaven's name could he wish to talk to Holmes about?

* * *

Sir Edward was some ten paces ahead when we reached the horse trap tucked in the shade of a great plane tree. He reached into the cab and with considerable difficulty brought out a large flat object, oblong and thin. The cloth fell away to reveal an oil-painting of three grandly-attired figures in a formal pose. I recognised two of them without difficulty, the late Great Queen as a young woman and next to her a pompous Emperor Napoleon III. They stared across the canvas at the third figure. The man wore a fez with a long black tassel and an imposing uniform with brilliant decorations. He was stretching out a magnificent sword for them to inspect.

I pointed at the exotic figure and said, 'Has the matter to do with this person? If so, he is…?'

'The Ottoman Sultan Abdul Mejid, long deceased. He is the father of Sultan Abd-ul-Hamid II, the current ruler of the Turkish Empire,' came the reply. 'It's not the man himself who concerns us, rather the weapon in his hand. I ask you to examine it closely.'

Holmes drew a silver and chrome magnifying glass from a pocket. He examined the sword in minute detail. Without explanation, Holmes transferred his scrutiny from the sword to the Sultan's features. Eventually he stepped back and replaced the glass in a pocket.

It was my turn. The sword appeared to be about four feet long and some four inches in width at the cross-guard. It bore a resemblance to the traditional Indian talwars with steel hilts and gold koftgari decoration I was accustomed to in the Indian subcontinent. On the Ottoman sword a gold cartouche was picked out in the centre of the blade at the start of a series of thin grooves. The hilt was of a black stone, the cross-bar decorated in relief in gold and black niello with a large emerald at the centre. A golden dragon-head formed the grip.

Grey resumed.

'This sword of state is called the Sword of Osman—after the founder of the Ottoman Dynasty. It's worn only at the investiture of a new sultan. In this painting the artist decided to depict the former sultan with the sword in his hand as a symbol of power, though in fact between inaugurations it never leaves Yildiz Palace where it's guarded behind heavy locked doors twenty-four hours a day.'

'Why should this weapon be of any interest to His Britannic Majesty's Government?' Holmes asked.

'Rumours are doing the rounds of a plot to steal it,' the Foreign Secretary replied. 'His Majesty's Government believes the matter must be taken very seriously.'

I frowned. The fate of an ancient sword hardly merited Holmes's journey from Sussex to London, or even from my medical practice just a mile or so away.

'Why would any such theft matter to England?' I pursued.

'Dr. Watson, I can assure you I wouldn't easily enter on a subterfuge to get Mr. Holmes to meet me here today if it were not of the utmost importance. He who holds the sword of state holds the key to power over the entire Turkish Empire. Its loss could mean the fall of the Sultan. If Abd-ul-Hamid falls, the ghost universe which is the present Ottoman Empire could totter and collapse like a house of cards.'

I fell silent, waiting for Holmes to respond. I judged the matter of little consequence, at most a quarrel among faraway peoples about whom we knew scarcely anything—and what we did know we didn't like.

For a moment Holmes appeared too absorbed with his own thoughts to give any immediate answer. Then to my dismay my comrade replied in the affirmative.

'Well, Sir Edward, we shall gladly accept the commission—on the grounds of all expenses being reimbursed by your Government. I believe my friend Dr. Watson would enjoy a week or two in Constantinople.'

England's Foreign Secretary gave a sigh of relief.

'You'll be fully reimbursed and more,' he replied. 'Incidentally, Mr. Holmes, it was your brother Mycroft who brought this matter to the attention of the Government. As you know, he sits at the nerve-centre of the Empire.'

The elder by seven years, Mycroft Holmes held an important if ill-defined position in His Majesty's Government. He dwelt in the self-contained world of Whitehall, his office almost equidistant from the War Department, the Foreign Office, Treasury and the Admiralty. His reach as puppet-master was immense.

The Foreign Secretary turned to look at me. 'Dr. Watson, you don't look convinced of the gravity of this mission. If there is a conspiracy and if it succeeds and the Sultanate collapses, the consequences could be cataclysmic. A mad quarrel would break out over the spoils. Among the powers of Europe Germany is best placed to rummage among the debris for advantage. She would gain direct access to the Euphrates. She would seize control of the Shatt El Arab. Even the heartlands of Islam would become hers. England's overland routes to India, vital to our control of the sub-Continent, would be endangered.'

'Why not give some small nod to the Kaiser's aspirations, Sir Edward?' I asked. 'Why not accommodate the wretched fellow? Let him have a few African colonies, some islands in the Pacific—and the commercial advantages you mention, a railway to Bagdad perhaps. *The Times* reports the Kaiser craves Agadir. Why not let him have it?'

'I'm asked that almost daily by "the German Party" in the House,' came the wry reply. 'His Majesty's Government has no strong objection to seeing the black, white and red flag flying over a few extra colonies in Africa, nor any special reason to deny the Kaiser a railway to Bagdad or a presence in the Pacific, if only that were enough. But as to Agadir becoming a German port—you of all people should not tolerate a division of German destroyers on the flank of our sea routes to India.'

He turned to look steadily at my comrade.

'A lot depends on you, Mr. Holmes,' he said, his voice low. 'Despite our scruples, we must sup with the Ottoman Devil, maintain the status quo for a while longer until the consequences for our Empire of a collapse of *his* Empire become clearer. All England should wish you well.'

Sir Edward waved at the horse-trap.

'Gentlemen, I'd offer you a ride to your next destination were I not in heavy demand at the House of Commons.'

With a further nod, he clambered into the carriage and gave a signal to the horse. Holmes called out, 'A request, Sir Edward—can you get a photographic enlargement of the sword to me? And a translation of the inscriptions?'

Sir Edward's free arm stretched upward in assent. The trap and painting clattered away along Albert Road at a good pace and rounded a bend. The Dark Continent with its great herds of elephants, the odd-toed ungulates on the Luangwa, the Tsavo man-eating lions, hippos on the Shire River, dust, blood, haunted baobab trees, Pygmies, sleeping sickness, malaria, snail fever, the smell of camp-fires long extinguished, all would have to wait.

Ahead of us lay a vast Mussulman dynastic Empire more than six centuries old. As a youth I had been entranced by oriental paintings in the National Gallery, in particular an oil of the massed beauty of the Harem women, a scene to rival the pages of the *Thousand Nights And A Night*, the silk and satin of the dresses sparkling with jewellery, the lines of black eunuchs, a sultan in scarlet robes edged with sable, a diamond-studded dagger at his waist. Instead of natives hiding in impenetrable bamboo there would be minarets amid gigantic black-green cypresses, bazaars, dervishes in sugar-coned hats, men in pumpkin-shaped turbans like giant white tomatoes and pashas staring out over the deep blue Sea of the Golden Horn wearing fezzes bright as poppy fields. At least my new camera and a magnificent new pair of powerful Ross 12X military binoculars would be of use anywhere.

* * *

The following day Holmes forwarded a letter from his brother Mycroft to my Chambers. It began, 'Dear Sherlock, I am delighted to hear the Foreign Secretary has engaged you on the Ottoman case. Your time will not be misspent. This is more than a chivalric emprise. England as the *Gouvernante* of the Levant has her obligations and interests to protect. The great trade routes of east and west, Peking, Samarkand, Kieff, Zanzibar, Vienna, all converge upon Constantinople. On your arrival in the heart of the Ottoman Empire you will find intrigue, counter-intrigue, lies, deceit, cupidity and malicious gossip. Every quarter of the city is honeycombed with foreign agents, some political, many economic. They and counter-agents are numerous as cockroaches, all spying on each other. All have washed up in Constantinople seeking

31

concessions—telegraphs, railways, bridges, banks. Some are friendly towards Britain, some are certainly not.

'A dragoman by the name of Eric Shelmerdine will be waiting for you at the Vinegar Sellers' wharf when you step ashore. He is Levantine or Armenian, I'm not clear which. Useful name, Eric. Eric to the English, Éric to the French, Erich to the Kaiser's men, Erik to the Hungarians. He purports to be a correspondent for the *Augsburger Allgemeine Zeitung* and *Pesti Naplo* but the majority of his pay comes from the treasuries of half a dozen Powers—one being England. He is acquainted with the hubble-bubble pipe servants of every Pasha in Pera. In no time the telegraph wires buzz and their masters' plots and plans are transmitted to us days in advance of (and far more truthful than) official reports.

'There are two contending groups who might wish to steal the Sword of Osman, and bring about Sultan Abd-ul-Hamid's overthrow. One is based in Salonika, initiated eight years ago by students at the Imperial Medical Academy. They call themselves "The Young Turks" (the 'Young' is a misnomer) and are led by a gentleman bearing the name Bahaeddin Shakir.'

Our adventure began to seem real.

'Their rival group is the League of Private Initiative and Decentralization, led by a prince in exile by the name of Sabahedrinne. His headquarters are in Paris, in a girls' school (the headmistress occupies the room next door). The communications network is a cubbyhole for a telephone operator, the chancellery a single typist, and yet...and yet... it is not beyond fantastic that from such lowly beginnings either enterprise could overthrow the world's strongest dictatorship.'

This was followed by a not-especially-complimentary description of the Ottoman Sultan. 'Abd-ul-Hamid II is a paragon of Oriental intriguers and dissimulators, less a bejewelled arachnid than a poisonous plant which cannot move to escape his predators. He is like the woody vine Aristolochia whose leaves are eaten by the larvae of swallowtail butterflies, thus making themselves unpalatable to their own predators. In earlier times a ruler of the Ottoman Empire would buckle on a sword and lead his troops into the fray. No longer. The ruler of a great empire sits in his Palace trembling like an aspen. There was a time Abd-ul-Hamid frequented the cafés on the Bosphorus incognito, with no fear the coffee would be poisoned. Now, the most elaborate precautions are taken with his food. Meals are cooked in kitchens with iron doors and barred windows and brought to him by officials in gold-embroidered uniforms wheeling a trolley containing the Imperial Dinner service. Each dish must be tasted by the Guardian of the Sultan's Health and Life who, it's said, tests it more on cats and dogs than himself. Abd-ul-Hamid prefers a humble stuffed marrow and cucumber to the elaborate concoctions his Greek chef can prepare. The taste of poison in such simple fare would be immediate.

'*Amusante?* It may pay to bear in mind there is only one punishment in his code. Death by strangulation or death by drowning, tied in a sack at the end of a grapnel and hurled into the Bosphorus, often after days or weeks of the most unbearable torture.'

As to the Sultan's paranoia, 'Year on year there's a steady growth in the number of his spies, known as *djournals*. Greeks, Hebrews, Armenians, Syrians and Levantines alike, they are thought to total as many as the foreign spies and sympathizers infesting Petersburg—more than 20,000. Almost every shop and nargile café in Stamboul is run by them. Almost every customer is a *djournal* too. We joke that when two Jews get together they build three synagogues. In popular belief, if three Turkish subjects are seen together one at least is certain to be a spy. Whenever you see two perfectly respectable men conversing they will instantly cease conversation if a third person draws near.

'There is a strong belief in the Evil Eye. The blue eye of the Frank (their term for all Europeans) is considered especially malign and sinister. What they will make of the colour of your eyes, Sherlock, I dare not think. As to the customs of the Turk, do not cross your feet at mealtimes, it is disrespectful to the table. Do not praise any item for as often as not it will be pressed into your hand—but not from generosity. Your praise has brought the Evil Eye upon it. It would bring bad luck to the owner if it were kept. Therefore you might make an exception to the rule and fulsomely admire a few Chinese vases and some Longquan celadon bowls, the spoils of centuries-long exchanges of gifts between Chinese emperors and Ottoman sultans. A few top class Chinese artefacts would sit well in the interior of the Diogenes Club. Ditto the Galata Bridge. An extra bridge across the Thames at The Temple would make access to the premises much easier for our legal fraternity (especially in their cups).'

The mention of the Diogenes made me smile. I recalled Holmes's description of his brother's favourite haven: 'There are many men in London who, some from shyness, some from misanthropy, have no wish for the company of their fellows. Yet they are not averse to comfortable chairs and the latest periodicals. No member is permitted to take the least notice of any other one. Save in the Stranger's Room, no talking is, under any circumstances, allowed, and three offences, if brought to the notice of the committee, render the talker liable to expulsion.'

There was no danger I would be invited to apply for membership—or accept if the offer were made.

I returned to the Mycroft letter.

'Cuisine: for centuries the Spice Routes from Asia have been under the complete control of the Sultanate. Carts rumble daily into the Palace, loaded with conserves of almonds, pistachios, ginger, hazelnuts, orange-peel, aloes, coffee, and of course Rahat Lokum forged from the pulp of white grapes or mulberries. The demands of Yildiz are voracious—butter from Moldavia via the Black Sea, great quantities of plums, dates and prunes shipped in from Egypt. Honeys are brought from Rumania and Hungary. The purest comes from the Isle of Crete and is reserved for the Sultan himself. Turkish delicacies make even Dr. Watson's favourite Sussex Puddle puddings or the roast meats at Simpson's Grand Divan Tavern seem as bland and commonplace as brown Windsor soup and boiled plaice. For the best Rahat Lokum you should certainly visit Hadji Bekir's Lumps of Delight factory, a small room near the Galata Bridge head.

And of course you must sample the Turkish milk desserts—the muhallebi.

'May I ask you to do me a favour and go to the Spice Market. Please bring back a few packages of saffron and my favourite Kofte Bahari—a mix of coriander, black pepper, cloves, bay leaves and wild thyme.'

* * *

That evening I took a late walk to the day-and-night Post Office on the ground floor of Morley's Hotel at Charing Cross to post my letter to Pretorius.

Chapter III

We Prepare For Constantinople

LETTERS were being composed and circulated thick and fast. One in Edward Grey's spidery writing was sent on to me from Holmes's bee-farm.

FOREIGN OFFICE
June 6, 1906

'My dear Mr. Holmes,— at my suggestion Haldane, the Secretary of State for War, has offered to put *HMS Dreadnought* at your disposal. It suits his convenience. She needs to complete her sea-trials and gunnery. The manufacturers claim her new steam turbines and four propeller shafts give her a speed of 21 knots, 3 knots faster than battleships with traditional piston engines. The turbines as well as her gunnery need testing almost to destruction. Haldane was going to send her to the West Indies but he too has concerns about the Kaiser's bellicose eye on our shipping lanes to Asia. If you board *Dreadnought* at Gibraltar she will carry you to the Eastern Mediterranean.

'I suggest you disguise your identity almost from the

minute you leave England. I have therefore arranged for the cost of authentic naval uniforms—working dress and full dress—and other accoutrements (including dress swords) to be covered by His Majesty's Government. If your tailors pass your measurements to Gieves, Matthews & Seagroves, or if you drop by in person, they will provide everything. They fitted out the last person we sent undercover to Constantinople in a khaki garb, something between that of a Colonel and Brigadier. He posed as an Army doctor intent on studying the use of vegetables in Ottoman medicine but never made it back.

'No doubt the Gieves people will remind you they dressed Stanley head to toe for his trek to the shores of Lake Tanganyika in search of Livingstone, just as when you collect your train tickets to Gibraltar from Thomas Cook & Son they will inform you they conveyed the relief force sent to Khartoum to rescue General 'Chinese' Gordon in 1884. Gieves is a centre of military gossip the equal of the In & Out Club so we have hinted your destination might be the Gold Coast.'

I settled down in my armchair to read the final page.

'I must repeat that if the plotters manage to steal the Sword of Osman they will make tremendous use of it in the Sultan's overthrow. Dr. Watson might ask why England should not stand aside and allow the *ad hoc* empire to be overthrown as a consequence of its own weight of corruption and misgovernment. After all, we have never guaranteed Turkey's regions and we do not intend to. I reply, if England intervenes we shall be seen to do so from a position of insatiable greed for possessions. On the other hand, if we stand aside and watch the Sultan overthrown and the High Divan collapse England will be isolated and discredited, hated by those we refused to help, despised by others. The fall of the Sultan and his detestable camarilla may liberate forces which none of us can foresee. None of the Great Powers is *désintéressé*. A European war could break out for which the one certain outcome would be six skeletons sitting around the peace table surrounded by a vast wasteland. For these reasons HMG (except for an energetic minority of the Cabinet) believes it is vital for the time being to preserve the integrity of the Ottoman Empire.

'Abd-ul-Hamid's vast empire continues to crumble around him. Centuries of malign neglect of the Ottoman provinces have brought such chaos that if the Empire falls it would take a Cromwell, a Napoleon, or above all an Ivan the Terrible to bring order and discipline. Three million Greeks, the million Armenians and the three-quarters of a million Bulgarians, not forgetting the quarter-million Jews, all want release from Ottoman dominion. However, history dictates that, bad as despotism is, the first-fruits of the overthrow of tyranny are not love and liberty. Perverse consequences and unintended outcomes are the rule.

'As to the custom of presenting gifts to His Imperial Majesty, a parcel will be delivered to Dr. Watson's premises before you set off. Some rolls of Offenbach. The Sultan plays such tunes endlessly on his pianola. And separately, at the Sultan's request, the most modern rifle of British manufacture.'

The letter came to a personal and lyrical end: 'I hope Dr. Watson as a keen fisherman will one day accept an invitation to my estate at Fallodon. We shall take our wet fly to the rivers of the North, the Lochy, the Cassley, the Helmsdale and the Findhorn. I would look forward to it very much. When I walk in a fine March wind and watch the ripples on a river and wonder if I could put a salmon fly as far as the opposite bank, I look God in the face and am refreshed._Yours sincerely, E. Grey'

There was a postscript: 'In addition to the gifts for the Sultan the Commodore of *HMS Dreadnought* will arrange for delivery of a specially-bound copy of *The Return of Sherlock Holmes* to His Imperial Majesty with our own Imperial Majesty's compliments.'

* * *

I returned the pages to the envelope. The grandfather clock in my waiting room struck the half-hour. A locum could attend to the remaining patients. I set off for George Street for a first appointment with the military tailors.

On my arrival at Gieves a wave of nostalgia washed through me. Nothing had changed since I visited the warren of stairs and rooms years before, an Army surgeon at Netley. Ahead of me at the time lay a stint in the blistering heat of the North-West Frontier, a succession of punitive expeditions against offending Pathans, the Second Anglo-Afghan War, my disabling wound from a Jezail bullet at the Battle of Maiwand, enteric fever, and a final return to Portsmouth jetty on the *Orontes*.

An elderly tailor approached. He stopped a few feet away and looked me over carefully, one finger to his mouth. A pair of cutting scissors dangled from a thumb. After a moment he put the scissors down and frowned at the appointment card.

'Surgeon Lieutenant Samuel Learson,' he said slowly. He looked back up at me. 'Learson,' he repeated. He shook his head. 'Sir, thick neck, that strongly built man square jaw of yours, length of inside leg, and dropping seven and a half pounds off your weight... if the name Learson was not clearly written here I'd swear you were the young medical officer who came here in '79. A John something...ah! Watson, I recall.'

Twenty minutes later he said, 'Did you know that when Stanley greeted Livingstone he found the Scottish Congregationalist wearing a blue Gieves Consular hat?'—the very tale he'd told when fitting me out for India twenty-seven years earlier.

* * *

Five days and two fittings later the naval uniforms together with the ceremonial swords and two greatcoats were delivered to my premises by a smart coach. The outfits also included a pea coat each—short double-breasted jacket made of coarse wool with six brass buttons inscribed with anchors. I tried on the dress uniform. The trousers were tight, with side pockets and fob pocket on the jacket. On Mycroft's instructions Gieves had supplied swords dating back to the reign of the late Great Queen when we might first have attained officer rank. The blades were about 30 inches in length, with a slight curve. A good amount of gilt remained to the hilts.

I turned to the working dress. Holmes as Commander had three gold cuff bands with white between them. Mine as a Naval Surgeon had two gold cuff bands separated by the Surgeon's red distinction stripe. Neither uniform bore the executive curl, the small loop on the top rim of cuff lace or shoulder tab. This insignia would, have put us in the chain of command over the ship or crew, giving us an authority and visibility we didn't wish for. The absence of the curl would help explain the lack of knowledge expected of an experienced seaman officer while not precluding us from holding the King's Commission.

To an Army man the etiquette of the Senior Service was deeply confusing. I was going to need guidance in the matter of protocol. A private note from the Commodore of *HMS Dreadnought* supplied it:

'Dear Dr. Watson, I and my crew look forward to your arrival aboard. Officially we are to conduct running trials and test our main guns and anti-torpedo boat defensive armament en route to the West Indies. As far as the world is concerned that's where we shall be going, but (as you know) both the Secretary of State for War and the Foreign Secretary are alarmed at the intensification of interest from the Kaiser into Ottoman affairs. German hegemony of any sort in the Near East could seriously impair our ability to use those sea routes in times of war, including access to the Suez Canal. Therefore, rather than sailing to the West Indies we shall steam in the greatest secrecy from Gibraltar to Turkey in record time—aided by the fact the seawater flow from Gib is eastward in the Strait's surface waters. We shall plan our arrival in Constantinople just before dawn to make greater impact on the Diplomatic community in Pera when it takes its first yawn of the day and glances out of the window. Only the Sultan himself will be informed of the exact time of our arrival.

'By now Gieves will have made your uniforms, both working dress and full dress according to regulations, including sword knots etc. Uniforms should be worn except when engaged in activities such as sport for which uniform would be inappropriate. Meetings with the Sultan or Grand Vizier will merit full dress (don't forget the swords).

'In your instance, as a Surgeon Lieutenant, you should learn the different style of salute. Naval surgeons do not stand for the loyal toast. Also, although Royal Navy medical officers are qualified doctors, they do not use the Dr. prefix.'

The letter was signed Reginald Bacon.

A few days later, a brevet-major from the India 2nd Battalion by the name of Crum, formerly of the King's Royal Rifle Corps, visited me with a package. Crum was a fine old soldier who had seen much of the world. Among the gifts for the Sultan was a most unusual sniper rifle, a modified, lengthened Short Magazine Lee Enfield produced by Parker Hale in the heart of Birmingham's Gun Quarter. It came with a dozen boxes of cartridges and a state-of-the-art Karl Kahles Telorar rifle scope. The package had been specially put together by the leading ballistician, Sir Charles Ross, 9th Baronet, owner of vast estates in Scotland. A note said the rounds had been engineered to achieve a muzzle velocity of over 2800 feet per second. Accompanying the rifle was a rubberised ghillie suit, a cloth garment covered in loose strips of burlap designed to resemble leaves and twigs. When manufactured correctly, the suit moved in the wind in the same way as the surrounding foliage.

* * *

Our departure was imminent. Holmes and I had already decided to use the pseudonyms we employed abroad once before: Holmes would return to being Naval Commander George Archibald Hewitt, the name of England's foremost forger. I would be Surgeon Lieutenant Samuel Learson, the country's most notorious safe-breaker.

Mycroft Holmes had taken charge of our arrangements. He wrote, 'Dear Dr. Watson, on the day and hour arranged, you will find a motor car brougham waiting at the kerb to take you to the station in time for the Continental Express. It will be driven by a jarvey with a heavy black cloak tipped at the collar with red. Allow time for the journey. The carriage will take you twenty minutes in the wrong direction to throw off any ill-wishers. The second first-class train carriage from the front is reserved for you and Sherlock. I enclose an albumen print by the Abdullah Frères of the Imperial Yıldız palace and the Hamidiye Mosque. At Sherlock's request, your dragoman will have a photographic enlargement of the sword at the ready on your arrival.'

* * *

The day arrived. I checked my watch against the chronopher one final time. A noisy Beeston-Humber Landaulette deposited me at Victoria Station. I was looking forward to the days aboard *HMS Dreadnought*, during which I might be able to write up a case or two. The choice would be difficult. In the meantime I joined a long queue at W.H. Smith's to purchase a supply of reading for the journey to Gibraltar.

Half an hour later I settled opposite Holmes into the comfortable First Class carriage aboard *The Jewel of the Weald*. I was extremely flustered due to an uncomfortable encounter with a clergyman. I have often related how my former comrade changed his colours as readily as the chameleon. Clerics were his speciality—in *A Scandal In Bohemia* Holmes disguised himself as a simple Nonconformist preacher in his effort to outwit the remarkable adventuress Irene Adler. I wrote at the time:

> '*His broad black hat, his baggy trousers, his white tie, his sympathetic smile, and general look of peering and benevolent curiosity... It was not merely that Holmes changed his*

costume. His expression, his manner, his very soul seemed to vary...'

When I hurried across Victoria station towards our carriage with my bundles and the day's *Globe*, *Pall Mall*, and *St. James's* I came across the identical apparition of the Nonconformist preacher with the identical sympathetic smile and general look of peering and benevolent curiosity.

I recalled Holmes saying 'It is the first quality of a criminal investigator that he should see through a disguise'.

I determined to unmask my friend there and then, only to find myself obliged to pay a loitering street Arab sixpence to retrieve a genuine prelate's hat and stick from the railway track to which had I dispatched them, yelling out 'You can't fool me thrice, sir!'.

On the dot of 11 o'clock, and much to my relief, the engine driver pulled the air whistle. Doors slammed. Steam was applied to the reciprocating pistons, giving life to the 4-4-0 wheels. With a deafening noise the monster began to hurl itself forward. A helpful Mr. Paul Smith at Thomas Cook's had told us the journey would last one hundred and four hours. Our first meal would be aboard the Dover-Boulogne ferry. Beyond lay Paris and Madrid. Then Algeciras and the steamer to Gibraltar.

I leaned towards Holmes, mischievously intending to enquire whether he'd remembered to bring his Legion of Honour Grand Croix to impress the Sultan, but was met with one of Holmes's most remarkable characteristics, the power to throw his brain out of action. With the unusual remark 'Watson, I've had quite enough of Petrarch for one day', my old friend snatched a pair of black night-spectacles from a pocket sewed inside his cavernous coat and popped them on his nose. He stretched out his long, thin legs, loosened his cravat, and lay as dead.

The train gathered speed, clacking its way across the Thames. Victoria Station fell back. I turned my attention to the outside world. St. Paul's Cathedral came into view, 365 feet high. A cloud-burst earlier that morning had washed the smoke and dust out of the air so that even at a distance the gilt cross sparkled in the sunshine. Spires, dwarfed by the dome, stood out with unnatural clarity.

I surrounded myself with a cloud of newspapers until at last, saturated with the events of the day, I tossed them to one side and stared at my sleeping friend. Next to Holmes lay a long cherry-wood pipe and his favourite clay pipe, a box of vestas, and a pouch with Grosvenor tobacco mixture (at eightpence an ounce). He had opted for a rare Poshteen Long Coat. He had worn it last in our encounter with the ruthless Empire Loyalists of the Kipling League and their President, David Siviter, in *The Case of the Dead Boer at Scotney Castle* some two years earlier. No-one would accuse Holmes of foppishness. The bulky piece with its many flaps and pockets was accompanied by a regrettable common-or-garden ear-flapped travelling cap showing signs of savage attack by moths, no respecters of ancient relics.

Beside me was a heavily-sealed document 'for the attention of Commander Hewitt' delivered to the train and passed to me by Holmes with the words 'Do oblige me when you have time'. The succinct address 'Bankside' indicated it had been written by Mycroft Holmes in the privacy of the Diogenes Club.

I lit a lunkah and began to read.

'Dear Sherlock, by now you will be boarding the express train to Dover, engaged in a task as important as any you have undertaken. Your destination Constantinople—often referred to as 'Stamboul'—has been called empress of the world, a city of beauty and tragedy, where a man's ancestry is proclaimed by the colour of his trousers—Turks red, Greeks black, Jews blue, Armenians violet. Turkey is more an Asiatic power than a European one.

'First, a cautionary word on wearing naval officers' uniforms. The Civil Service is in the throes of drawing up a new Convention regarding the status of wartime spies. Ch.11, Article 29 will state a person is considered a spy who acts clandestinely or on false pretences, infiltrates enemy lines with the intention of acquiring intelligence and communicating it to the belligerent during times of war. You should, therefore, be aware that if war breaks out during your stay in Turkey, and the Ottomans are on the other side, you will be executed. Now you know of this risk no-one will hold it against you or Dr. Watson if you spend a pleasant hour or two at Dover Castle followed by a six-course dinner courtesy of His Majesty on the next train back to Victoria. Otherwise read on.

'The Sultan is a bottomless pit of falsehood and fraud

who will fulfil nothing except under force or the proximate use of force. The East is, and ever was from times immemorial, the land of the most striking contradictions. Venice in its darkest days was light and freedom compared to the cesspool of vice, decay and blood which is the Stamboul of today. Across the Ottoman Empire provinces which were once rich and fertile have returned to nearly the desolation of the desert, in parts a howling wilderness.

'Europe waits with bated breath for Ottoman rule to collapse. St. Petersburg and Vienna bide their time like crows on a fence post. Berlin maintains a ship anchored for months at a time in the harbour at Stamboul full of political and commercial spies masquerading as archaeologists and engineering geographers. We have good reason to believe the Kaiser signed a secret military convention with the Sultan when Abd-ul-Hamid hosted him in Constantinople eight years ago. If war breaks out between Germany and England, we will find the Turk on the other side. Why should this be of concern to London? Because when the Sick Man does collapse England must have her share of the spoils. Our power extends to the boundaries of even the farthest ocean. In Kipling's words, England holds Dominion over palm and pine. Our world-empire is an octopus with gigantic feelers stretching out over the habitable globe. Many economies including China and Siam are under our control.'

The letter went on, 'The Foreign Secretary is not the most sensitive barometer by which to read tendencies in foreign policy. His attention is fixed too hard on France, a corrupt and traditional enemy which to my mind remains of interest but no longer consequence. England herself is in urgent need of a Metternich, a Talleyrand, a blood-and-iron Bismarck, which Sir Edward is not. History may show the King's recent Entente with Paris was England's first blundering step to war with Germany. There is not enough dissimulation in Grey for a politician. Rather, he is an unpretending Englishman of country tastes, simple in word and thought, good at fishing and learned in sparrows. Perhaps I'm being unfair—there is in great affairs so much less in the minds of the chief actors than in the minds of the event. In emergencies we discover we are the puppets of the past which, of a sudden, pulls the unseen wires and determines the action.'

I resented Mycroft's mild contempt for Sir Edward's 'country tastes'. The Foreign Secretary was a man after my own heart.

A chilling analysis unfolded.

'When the next crisis comes we shall find the war-chariots' reins not in Whitehall but Wilhelmstraße. There is a good deal of gunpowder lying about in Berlin waiting for a spark, its ruler keen to settle differences sword in hand. The mischief-makers' time is coming, *ohne Hast, aber ohne Rast*—without haste, but without rest. The gifts of patience, forbearance and tact may be invaluable for the conduct of delicate negotiations but Germany is not a wilting lily. She is a walnut which it will require a hammer to crack. Grey will be powerless to prevent the shipwreck which is now inevitable It only takes one to make a quarrel; it needs two to preserve the peace.'

The above is expressed in the deepest confidence that it will find a place in your and Dr. Watson's minds and not an inch further. This was followed by the cautionary words, 'I need not remind you, dear brother, I have a comfortable chair here in Whitehall. With time and usage it has taken on the curvature of my back (and rump) and I hope to remain in it for many moons to come. After you have fully absorbed its content burn this document.'

'Burn this document' was heavily underlined.

The last of London was now behind us. We were puffing towards the forbidding bulwark of the White Cliffs and, beyond, the English Channel and France. I put Mycroft's letter away and pulled my tin box from the rack, riffling through case-notes yet to see the light of day.

I smoothed out the pages and spread them on the seat beside me.

* * *

Days and nights passed. We rattled through France at forty miles an hour aboard a succession of wind-splitting 'pig-nosed' trains. A hundred hamlets passed by in a blur. Restaurant cars serving hearty food and fine wines ameliorated the long evenings. I picked up and put down and picked up *The Best Letters of Lady Mary Wortley Montagu* and *Diary of an Idle Woman in Constantinople*. I alternated staring out of the carriage windows with seizing the chance when Holmes dozed to continue my transcriptions. Finally we were within shot of Algeciras. Beyond lay Gibraltar. Soon we would be sailing through the Mediterranean into the Aegean Sea.

Hundreds of miles into our journey, irrevocably committed to our new adventure, I returned to the final paragraph of Mycroft's letter.

'I think Sir Edward and I have covered the politics enough. You will be received by the Sultan at Yildiz Palace in your guise as naval emissaries acting on requests from the Royal Botanical Gardens and the Zoological Society Gardens. You will not be shown the Sultan's Harem, the Harem-i Hümâyûn. English feet have stamped their mark on much of the world, Whymper's on the peak of the Matterhorn, Speke's at the source of the Nile, but along with the North Pole and the summit of Everest the Harem remains among the few places on earth no English (or American) foot has yet trod.'

Chapter IV

We Board HMS Dreadnought

I AWOKE next morning to find Holmes changing into the Commander's uniform and pulling on his boots. I flung myself into the Surgeon Lieutenant's dress uniform. The train slowed and came to a halt at our final station, Algeciras. I jumped out. Across the bay we could see the rock of Gibraltar towering above the sea.

A porter unloaded our luggage and placed it alongside us in a cab to the harbour. Holmes murmured, 'Watson, I understand old Army habits die hard but if you are to pass as a naval officer you must rid yourself of the custom of placing a handkerchief in your sleeve. It might well be remarked upon by the crew.'

The paddle-steamer *Elvira* was waiting to take us across the water to the spanking new Edward VII Dock. To reinforce our subterfuge we made a point of going at once to inspect the pile of Wardian cases delivered to the dockside ahead of us. The sealed glass protected plants imported from faraway regions. Several cases were filled with plants personally requested by the Sultan from the Royal Botanical Gardens—bulbs of an exotic lily discovered in the I'Chang gorges of the Yangtze River in 1881, cushion plants with their origins in the Peruvian Andes, and the gigantic Victoria regia lily, brought to England from the shallow waters of a river in British Guiana.

The mighty *HMS Dreadnought*, built at a cost of £1,783,883, was to become the defining artefact of the Age. Colourful flags flew from her masts and sternpost. Before boarding the battleship we collected a package of letters forwarded to us care of Messrs. Cox & Co's correspondent bank in Gibraltar. One letter was directed at Holmes from his brother, the other to me from the Congo. I retained considerable loyalty to Cox's. The Bank served me well in India and during a short stint in the barrier-colony of Burma.

With the letters in our pockets we went aboard and were shown to our cabins. I unpacked and opened Pretorius's letter. It had passed mine in transit, probably at one or other end of the Suez Canal. He was anticipating my arrival with a keen interest, and that of my 'magic box' (the medicine chest).

I put the document down with a heavy heart. Our plans would now have to take their place on the back-burner.

Well before dawn a Yeoman boarded with the final telegraphs from the Signal Tower. *Dreadnought* cast off her moorings and slowly swung away from land. I stared out of the porthole. Even in the dark, a large patriotic crowd gathered along the dock to watch the impressive sight. The great vessel gathered speed. She cast off the tugs and we steamed away as though on a course for the Caribbean. At our back lay the Mediterranean, formed where Africa crashes against Eurasia, a million square miles of sea of a shape and clime almost perfect for the development of civilization. Out of sight of land we would make an about turn, steam through the Pillars of Hercules and run as secretly as possible to the shores of Stamboul, 2,101 nautical miles distant.

* * *

Dinners aboard were remarkably friendly affairs. The pudding served, Commodore Bacon would give orders no-one was to enter the Wardroom without his express permission unless war was declared. The first night he raised a glass and addressed Holmes and me with 'I advise you to snatch whatever sleep you can. We shall be steaming at 21 knots, testing the new Parsons turbines to the limit, big guns and torpedoes too. There'll be long range battle practices, short range battle practices, night battle practices and several advanced day battle practices—firing in indirect mode through smoke screens. We'll also be testing whether our torpedoes can hit a target at 4,000 yards.'

He planned at least one experimental practice, to explore *Dreadnought's* ability to keep on target during a radical turn. 'Nevertheless, gentlemen, despite all the action we should have time for the occasional glass of port and conversation.'

The Commodore looked across at Holmes and me. In a lowered voice he said, 'Only the officers around this table know who you are. The crew have been told you're visiting Anatolia and East Thrace to purchase exotic birds for the Zoological Society of London and rare plants for the Royal Botanical Gardens at Kew. The large pile of Wardian cases has impressed them no end. I think it best from now on if we become accustomed to using your pseudonyms. Once we've coaled and my men go ashore it's not unknown for them to take a Mastika or a Raki or two—banana raki, mustard raki, pomegranate raki, aniseed raki—or other tongue-loosening concoctions. Everyone aboard has arrived within the last couple of months or so from other ships of the line. I suggest you stay entirely non-committal if asked where and on which ships you've served, in case you give yourselves away.'

Thus eight days passed with tranquil intervals between the uproar of the great guns and torpedo-firing. I spent hours with the binoculars purchased for the Congo trip staring at passing islands wreathed in the legends of noble Hector, brave Achilles and cunning Ulysses.

On the last evening during drinks in the Mess a signal was brought in by a Petty Officer and handed to the Commodore who took us to one side.

'The Sultan of Turkey will come aboard soon after we set anchor. I'll have to lay on a bit of pomp and ceremony and a display of uniforms. I take it you would like to meet the Khan of Khans and his party? If you come to the Gun-deck we'll introduce you...'

Almost rudely, Holmes interrupted.

'Thank you no, Commodore. The Lieutenant and I intend to go ashore at precisely that moment if you'll make the arrangements.'

Without further explanation, Holmes said his goodnights and strode away.

Perplexed, I hurried after him.

'Holmes, I thought our aim was to meet the Sultan. Why are we passing up such a golden opportunity?'

He waved a ciphered telegram at me.

'Neither the Sultan nor we should wish to meet amid the throng of international Press and a hundred cameras. Besides, Mycroft's agent has arranged a transport to take us to the Palace as soon as we can get ashore.'

* * *

The constellation Draco was still visible in the night sky when we dropped anchor. Across the Sea of Marmara I could see a thousand sparkling lights. Stamboul, the arm of the peninsular, was now within range of our immense guns. Like the ashes of a phoenix, the Scott Eccles affair would have to lie awaiting rebirth as a fully-fledged Sherlock Holmes manifesto. The material was unusually extensive. I sat on the bunk staring at it. I supposed I could break the chronicle into two parts. There was a knock on the cabin door. It was a steward returning my freshly-ironed Surgeon Lieutenant's naval dress suit. The sword too had been polished and was returned with its scabbard.

As the sun rose, dark shapes around us suddenly became comprehensible. I climbed up to the Gun-deck. Our battleship was surrounded by the largest single assembly of warships I had ever seen. When we crept past the island of Malta by night, a Royal Navy squadron must have sailed out of Grand Harbour and fallen in behind us, accompanying us for the last fifteen hundred miles, unseen, swift and unlit. I counted 10 first-class battleships silhouetted against the pink sky, plus frigates, torpedo boat destroyers and various despatch vessels and depot ships and the great bulks of two armoured cruisers of 9800 tons, *HMS Lancaster* and *HMS*

Suffolk, castles of steel with fourteen six-inch guns and four-inch armour plate.

I stood with Holmes on *Dreadnought's* deck waiting for a pinnace from the dockyard to take us ashore. Great steamers from every country churned back and forth whistling incessantly. Across the shimmering waters of the Golden Horn richly painted private vessels with long up-curving prows carried distinguished passengers in the stern under silken canopies, the owner's rank dictating the number of oars. Nearby was a ship of the North German Lloyd line, the *S.S. Grosser Kurfürst*. Her decks and bridge were alive with the flashes of the sun reflecting from a hundred telescopes pointed in our direction.

By the harbour the creaking board-walk known as Galata Bridge bound Europe with Asia, Frank with Moslem, civilization with barbarism. Below and around it, tiny against the immensity of our battleship, barges plied for hire, darting about in every direction among lateen-rigged yawls and feluccas. In a high state of anticipation onlookers in turbans, keffiahs and fezzes, and Europeanised Turks in Stamboulines, moved along the bridge in a steady stream with the sedan-bearers. English couples en route to India with white umbrellas and puggried sun-hats wandered alongside veiled women with long draping mantles and ribboned panniers. Firemen carried large skins of water ready to dampen down any sudden conflagrations.

The roar of the crowds and the sudden flare of a beacon on the hillside announced the Sultan was about to leave his Palace. Through my binoculars I watched the open phaeton emerge at a trot from a huge gate, heading for the Imperial caique moored at Tersane. It was escorted by a detachment of the Twelfth Royal Lancers composed of Khurds and Anatolians. A living swarm of courtiers, eunuchs, household aides and panting pashas in heavy gold-embroidered uniforms ran alongside. An enthusiastic crowd of about fifty people waited at its waterfront destination ready to remove the horses and pull the coach the final hundred yards.

I heard Holmes's voice. There was tinge of urgency in it.

'Watson, are you ready? We must go.'

He gestured as though sweeping me to a gangplank. The steam pinnace had arrived, the name *Haroony* in English lettering still fresh on its bow. *Dreadnought's* crew briskly transferred the thirty or more wood-and-glass Wardian cases guising us as naval plant collectors.

I went to my cabin to pick up the Offenbach rolls and the Lee Enfield. Holmes and I each wedged under an arm a copy of Hooker's *On the Vegetation of the Galapagos Archipelago*, a study of the plants Charles Darwin brought back on the *Beagle*. The wind blew straight in from the distant isles of Greece as we went down a gangway and clambered aboard the waiting transport, an awkward manoeuvre in naval dress uniform and sword.

I used the binoculars to watch the Imperial caique setting out. The Sultan and four personages of his suite were seated on a dais in crimson-magenta velvet under a gold and purple canopy, rowed at an impressive pace by forty oarsmen dressed in white with blue, red-tasselled caps. The whole looked like a gigantic water-boatman on the surface of a pond. The royal turban-bearer followed the Sultan's caique in a smart, eighteen-oar ship's cutter, holding up one of three royal turbans ornamented with herons' feathers and huge jewelled aigrettes which he inclined to the right and left, acknowledging the prostrations and cheers of the onlookers on behalf of his Imperial master. He was followed by an ensemble of energetic musicians—two drums, flute, triangle and viola—standing at constant risk of tipping over the gunwale of their tiny craft.

We slowed to avoid our wake jolting the on-coming barge as it went on by. The caique presented a sight of Moghul-like magnificence. The Sultan wore a turban adorned with three upside-down aigrettes, the equivalent of crowns, reinforced with hooked gold chains, dancing with plumes sourced from half the globe—crested cranes, peacocks, herons, hawks, ostriches, and birds of paradise. Behind him, like a bulbous shadow, stood a gigantic Abyssinian of phenomenal stature, head abased, the innumerable chins melting into a mountain of flesh. He wore a huge hat in the shape of a sugar-loaf at a slant on the back of his head.

Minutes later the Imperial visitors stepped aboard *Dreadnought*. The heaviest guns ever mounted at sea began a 21-gun salute. Then it was the Turkish Navy's turn to commence their own deafening salute, gun for gun.

Holmes and I stepped ashore. A sudden roar from the assembly on Galata Bridge drowned out the wailing note of the water-carriers and the raucous shouts of the Khurdish porters. We swung round to look. A submarine had bobbed up by the bridge. The Turks do not applaud with their hands.

Their approval was signified by the hum of hundreds and hundreds of voices, a noise like the purring of a thousand cats. The telescopes aboard the *S. S. Grosser Kurfürst* swung to study the jouncing craft with the British navy White Ensign flapping in the slight breeze.

* * *

The steel wheels made a familiar growling sound as a Clarence emerged from the shade of a high wall at the Vinegar Sellers' wharf. Behind it came a heavy two-wheeled cart to transport the pile of Wardian boxes, pulled by a jink-backed mare with feet like butcher's blocks. I had seen this condition often when animals suffer an extreme wrench below the short ribs from a slip, or more often from being made to drag too great a burden. Both conveyances had a horseshoe with a central glass 'evil eye' dangling from the side to ward off bad things.

A man jumped out of the Clarence and greeted us. It was Mycroft's man, Eric Shelmerdine. His English was so perfect he might have attended Eton College.

'I've obtained an audience for you from His Imperial Majesty, the Padishah,' he told us in a whisper as we climbed into the coach. 'I'm to take you to him straight away.'

'Which will be where?' I asked, wondering how long we would have to wait, knowing the glistering 'Padishah' and his entourage were behind us aboard *Dreadnought*.

He pointed.

'Up there. At Yildiz Kiosk. The Sultan's favourite palace. Despite the heat I advise you to put on your coats and keep them buttoned up. We get there by a dusty track.'

The dragoman pulled up the carriage windows on either side, tapped on the wood-work, and away we rattled as fast as the horse could go.

Conversationally I began, 'I believe you write for the newspapers?'

'Yes,' he affirmed. 'Mostly obituaries.'

'Obituaries!' I blurted.

'Sometimes I do a piece on the Sultan's activities.'

'And you are given a free hand?' I enquired.

'Of course not,' he replied cheerfully. 'This is Turkey. All local papers receive subsidies from Yildiz.'

'Therefore,' I pursued, 'you cannot criticise the Sultan?'

'Great Scot no!' he exclaimed. 'When His Majesty's name is mentioned we speak in superlatives. Last week I referred to him as 'recognised to be the wisest ruler in Europe'. Next week…'

He paused, calculating.

'…it'll soon be time once more for 'the greatest Sovereign who ever girded on the Sword of Osman'. After that it may return to the old standby, 'a model ruler, one whose good actions are so numerous that if those performed in a single day were all printed, the columns of all the newspapers in the Empire would be insufficient to report them'.'

He pointed to the camera at my side.

'What a wonderful Quarter Plate.'

His hand went to a pocket.

'That reminds me, I have a photograph for you. An enlargement of the Sword blade as requested.'

The dragoman stared at my new camera with a dubious expression.

'And you intend to photograph 'the Mountain Eagle, the one whose exploits outshine every other monarch'?'

'I do,' I replied. 'Unless you think he…?'

'Far from it,' he replied. 'He'll be delighted. The Sultan will save you the bother of carrying your camera all the way back to *HMS Dreadnought*. He takes it for granted that anything which attracts him is being given to him—daggers, jewel-encrusted ornaments. The Sultan-Caliph will be very grateful for…' he bent forward to get closer to my camera, '… the latest Lizars.'

Conversation lapsed. I looked out of the carriage at the passing sights. Small, clean-eared Arabian horses plunged their faces into great deep basins, lustily lapping the water. Rows of fruit-shops offered apricots, cherries and plums from large baskets, and packages of young vine leaves used lavishly in Turkish cooking. A Cypress tree in the courtyard of a mosque and a stand of Oriental Plane, huge and old, had managed to survive a recent conflagration. The trees stood bereft of greenery, stately boles pitted and charred.

Our dragoman followed my gaze.

'As you see, fire is a great hazard in Stamboul.'

He pointed up the hill.

'That white tower has a perpetual watchman stationed in the turret to signal if a fire breaks out. At the first sign of fire drums are banged and guns fired and a coloured flag is raised to indicate the quarter. The firemen rush in with long iron hooks and pull down all the adjacent houses.'

'What's the local word for 'fire'?' I asked.

'*Yangin*,' came the reply.

'*Yangin*,' I repeated. It was my first Turkish word.

'Another fireman stands watch on the Yildiz clock tower,' our dragoman went on. Dropping his voice he murmured, 'They say the Sultan likes to take a rifle up there of an evening to indulge in what your Army calls the Mad Minute.'

I was familiar with the Mad Minute from my military training. It entailed firing a minimum of fifteen aimed bullets into a distant target within sixty seconds.

When the clatter of the wheels obscured his words from the driver, Shelmerdine added, 'The 'mad minute' here is like yours, with one important difference. The Sovereign of the House of Osman aims bullets at real people. With so much practice he has become a magnificent shot. I wager he would challenge you, Dr. Watson, for marksmanship with the rifle.'

He pointed at the lengthy bundle at my side.

'He'll soon master that. And,' he carried on slyly, looking at the boxes, 'the smokeless cartridges will be most useful. At present, everyone knows when the Sultan fires down on his subjects by the cloud of black-powder smoke rising from the spot.'

We drove past a dignified tomb surrounded by a complex of medreses and mosques. Other tombs were scattered among ancient Italian cypresses and nettle-trees. Storks wandered freely or nested on the domes.

In a louder voice Shelmerdine continued, 'Mr. Holmes, your brother has asked me to give you some background into the state of play here. You will find Yildiz Palace a strange and cosmopolitan landscape. The grooms are Arabs, the footmen English, German and French. The nurses are Armenian, the housemaids Russian, stewards Italian, janizaries Turkish. French is the first foreign language acquired by members of Turkey's elite. The rest speak Persian, Arabic, Greek, Judeo-Spanish, Armenian, Wallachian, English, Dutch, German, Italian, and Sclavonian.'

Shelmerdine described an empire in miniature populated with Sandali—black eunuchs whose genitalia had been entirely amputated—white eunuchs, harem women, some captured or purchased, some voluntarily entering a hotbed of plots and counter-plots, mystery and bribery in return for the chance of high rank and wealth. Until recently the Valide Sultan Rahime Perestu presided over them all as ruler of the Imperial Harem. She was the all-powerful foster-mother of the present Sultan, with her rooms always adjacent to her son's. The post was now vacant. 'Eighteen months ago the Valide Sultan took ill in her villa at Maçka and died. The Sultan felt her loss terribly. For one week the military band did not perform. At the time of her passing I wrote: 'The esteemed lady's luminous face, graciousness, delicate manner, and elegance inspired respect and affection in everyone's heart, so that all those living in the palace loved her deeply'.'

'She died of...?' I asked.

'Croup.'

'Croup?' I exclaimed, puzzled.

Croup was a respiratory condition almost only seen in children. Even in the very young it was seldom fatal.

Our dragoman nodded.

'Newspapers are under the strictest orders never to report a Royal Personage died from old age or assassination. No king, president or emperor dies by an assassin's knife, pistol or bomb. Empress Elizabeth wasn't really stabbed to death in Geneva by an Italian anarchist.'

'So how…?' I asked.

'Pneumonia.'

'And President McKinley?' Holmes asked.

'Anthrax. As to King Alexander and Queen Draga of Serbia two years ago, you would be wrong to assume they were killed by a fusillade of bullets.'

We looked at our dragoman expectantly.

'Indigestion. Simultaneously.'

Abd-ul-Hamid's succession was not without its difficulties, Shelmerdine continued. The Sultan was brought to the throne by the murder of his uncle and the deposing and imprisonment of his half-brother.

'As a result he is dominated by fears of conspiracy and revolt, and not without reason. Last year the Armenian Revolutionary Federation left a bomb for him outside the Yıldız Mosque. I was there. There was a huge explosion. People, phaetons and horses were blasted into the air but the Sultan survived. Since then he has become morbidly suspicious. He buries himself in his Palace, in the company of soothsayers, astrologers, courtiers and police informers. He appears in public as seldom as possible, and always heavily guarded by soldiers.'

Shelmerdine pointed down a side-street at an assembly

of parked vehicles identical to London's Metropolitan Police wagons.

'Those are everywhere, ready to make mass arrests if the people riot.'

We were now high up on the slope.

'I may not be a medical man, Dr. Watson,' the dragoman pursued, turning to me, 'but I'm not the only person to say God's Promise on Earth is sick in mind and body, obsessed with one idea, that of preserving his throne and his life. Wherever the Sultan sits he has advance notice of anyone coming in. Mirrors hang at every angle of the room. Every room has its cage of parrots which screech at the sight of strangers. Every door is lined with steel. He goes to bed only after the woman who shares his bed has searched every cranny for a hidden bomb. In knowledge of your own English Gunpowder Treason Plot he never sits in a room above a dungeon. Abd-ul-Hamid even keeps his own submarine down near the Dolma Baghchech Pier. When a fit of fear or superstition strikes the Commander of the Faithful and Successor of the Prophet of the Lord of the Universe, he hastens to the pier and stays the night submerged in his submarine a few miles out in the Sea of Marmara. He did so two days ago when news arrived from the Black Sea that a flock of purple-and-white hoopoes appeared at the very time the North Star was in alignment with the moon.'

Our guide pulled another photograph from his pocket. This time it was a fading picture of a submarine. He pointed at the waters below.

'Your English submarine down there is to be a replacement for this vessel, the Nordenfelt 11.'

Like the earlier enlargement of the Sword of Osman, the photograph was in sharp focus.

'Who took these?' I heard Holmes ask.

Shelmerdine pointed at himself.

'I did.'

Our interpreter resumed, 'As he grows older the Sultan's private horrors also grow, not least a horror of darkness. By night tortoises with oil lamps attached to their shells creep among the beds of flowers. The Great Lord is so terrified by the stillness that armed guards have to tramp ceaselessly up and down outside his bed-room. If eunuch or guard encounters the Sultan, they must shake his hand in a particular way, with a twist or crack of the fingers. Without that secret signal he's likely to pull out an automatic and kill them on the spot.'

Shelmerdine told us about a diver trying to reach a wreck just off Seraglio Point who signalled violently to be drawn back up. Once safely ashore the man explained in a voice quaking with terror he'd found himself among a great number of sacks on the bottom of the sea. Each contained the body of a woman standing upright, her hair swaying to and fro in the current.

We were approaching the Palace. Shelmerdine lowered his voice.

'Abd-ul-Hamid fritters away his days in intrigue. He bribes everyone he considers a likely enemy—soldiers, hodjas, imams. Dancing Dervishes. Softas. At least, he thinks he's bribing them. The money and jewels seldom reach their targets. They mostly remain in the pockets of the two chief Palace eunuchs.'

Our interpreter bent his head to look out of the carriage window. The first of the Imperial gates loomed, the fine portico flanked by sixteen columns of Bulgarian syenite. The bright muskets of a dozen sentinels rustled in salute as we drew near.

'The Great Khan is particularly sensitive right now. This month we've had an eclipse of the Moon, the flight of a shooting star, flashes of lightning, thunder as deafening as a battleship's biggest guns. Last week street dogs howled during the morning Ezan, the Islamic call to worship. To Ottomans these are omens spelling the death of someone of great importance. Abd-ul-Hamid fears it could be his.'

Our dragoman opened the carriage door and stepped out.

'Here I shall bid you adieu. You will find the Second Black Eunuch waiting for you just inside the gate. His name is Nadir Aga.'

'And the First Black Eunuch?' I called out.

'That's Djafer Aga, a pasha of three peacock tails. You saw him on the Imperial barge.'

He leaned in at the now-open window.

'Abd-ul-Hamid likes to be called "His Sublimity". Doesn't come easily to Englishmen's lips, does it! A last word. If there's any truth in the rumour about the sword my guess would be the conspirators are members of the Committee of Union and Progress. Half the Keepers of the Imperial night-ingales and parrots, the pipe-cleaners and coffee-makers, the sword-bearers and stirrup-holders are in the pay of the CUP. Even barbers who have no other function than to trim the Sultan's beard, every hair of which is reverentially preserved. If their leader Bahaeddin Shakir gains possession of the sword they could move against His Sublimity within days.'

He paused, looking hard at us.

'If that were to happen the CUP will throw their lot in with Berlin not London. You, sir...' at this he stared at Sherlock Holmes, '...may well be the Padishah's last hope.'

I leaned from the carriage window and dropped a few piastres into his hand as though we had hired him for the hour. With a loud *As-salamu alaykum* he turned away from the carriage. Holmes called after him, 'And you, sir, your religion?'

The answer came back in a whisper.

'I was born into the Mother Church of Christendom but,' and his voice dropped even lower, 'whichever suits the circumstance.'

At this he was gone, curiously diaphanous amid the cluster of flower-sellers, barbers and perfumers who importuned visitors from each side of the great gate.

We stepped out of the carriage.

Chapter V

We Meet The Khan Of Khans

INSIDE the great gate we were approached by the Second Black Eunuch, Nadir Aga. He led us towards our destination, the elaborately decorated Mabeyn Pavilion, the most important building of the Palace. Columns of porphyry, white-mottled verd-antique and stones stood in the most unlikely places surmounted with capitals appropriated from the fallen churches and tombs of Constantine and his descendants.

Holmes whispered, 'Watson, I'll be most obliged if you'll fix in your mind each detail of our journey through the Palace. It may come in useful.'

We padded behind the Second Black Eunuch, along corridors and up and down hidden stairways, through rooms with walls decorated with flintlock holster pistols. Kapıcı (doorkeepers) at every entrance hurriedly performed their duties as we approached. We passed through workshops manufacturing heavy silks with exotic names to match—kemha, kadife, çatma—lighter silks such as taffeta and seraser, a precious silk fabric woven with threads of gold and silver. In the gathering heat it felt a long walk to our destination. We glimpsed fretted fountains and gilded kiosks, scarlet, blue, yellow, brilliant lilac and mauve mingling in the wildest ways, the love of colour quite Indian. On we strode, past shade trees, bowers with ivy and wisterias, and lion statues, water pouring like near-silent roars from their mouths. I inhaled the soft perfume of honeysuckles and jessamines wafting from nearby parterres.

The Second Black Eunuch's pace slowed. We were nearing the Mabeyn Pavilion. Uncertain which of us was which, he addressed us together.

'Milords, the Sultan has provided a test. Mr. Holmes must prove beyond doubt he is the real Sherlock Holmes, Europe's greatest detective, and not a look-alike bent on His Imperial Majesty's destruction. It will be better for you both if Mr. Holmes passes the test by making the correct choice.'

* * *

We stepped through the Pavilion doorway like Alice following the White Rabbit. A window like a balcony jutted into the Royal Garden. A drugget covered the centre of the waxed oak floor. Four fair slaves moved around the room perfuming the air. The walls were arrayed with landscape paintings, interspersed by tiles put together to make whole murals of calligraphy. In a wall niche stood a painted grey pottery figure of an official of the Northern Wei Dynasty, brought from faraway Cathay, hands hidden within the sleeves rested atop a sheathed sword.

It was not the magnificence of the furnishings nor the beguiling female slaves which transfixed me. It was the three men seated on separate identical thrones. Each was an exact copy of each other, not only in their gorgeous attire and the jewelled orders on their breasts but in height, shape of nose, jaw and forehead, and colouration of eye. The trio peered back at us with a curiosity equal to our own. Each held a lance topped by a gold-plated brass ball with nine tails of yak or horse-hair suspended from it. Each wore an identical turban placed neatly above the ears, a straight cylinder of pasteboard about two feet high covered with muslin and then red fabric, and decorated with feathers and a band of gold. A bejewelled Turkish water-pipe, a nargileh, stood beside each man. At their waists were identical daggers with three pear-shaped emeralds.

We waited, staring at the trio until the slaves had filled the room with the scent of aloes-wood and amber. The silence was broken only by the continuous and gentle sounds of water tumbling from basin to basin of a white marble wall-fountain.

After a profound obeisance, the Second Black Eunuch bade us move forward to a place of honour in the corner of the room. As we did so, he whispered in my ear, 'Do not be surprised at the sight of three identical sultans before you. His Imperial Majesty, the Sultan us-Salatin, has fifteen doubles.'

As Nadir Aga ended this explanation the three sultans' hands rose in greeting. The Second Black Eunuch called out in a magniloquent voice, 'Whichever of you is Mr. Holmes must prove you are the world's most famous consulting detective with powers of observation far beyond the ordinary run of men. This is your test. You are required to identify which of those seated before you is the true Redresser of Wrongs, the Khan of Khans.'

I smiled. Patently the Palace had arranged to play an amusing trick. We had passed close by the ruler and his entourage on their way to *HMS Dreadnought*. Even now we could hear the distant rat-tat-tat of the 12lb anti-torpedo craft guns and the occasional thunder of the battleship's heavy guns as she waged mock battle against her sister ships for the Sultan's entertainment. It would be at least two hours before they could return to the Palace.

Noting my expression the Second Black Eunuch murmured, 'I can assure you the real Sultan rarely leaves Yildiz. He is here, now, in this room. One of the three before you is God's Promise on Earth. Two of them—like the surrogate who at this moment stands on the bridge of the English battleship—are not.'

Without a second's hesitation Holmes indicated the figure on the right.

* * *

With a wave of the genuine Sultan's hand the two doppelgänger left, carrying their glittering water-pipes. We were now alone with the 34th sultan of the Ottoman Empire, the 99th caliph of Islam, ruler of a vast Asiatic empire. Our inability to speak Turkish or Persian was absolute and would require an interpreter. I wondered how we would communicate when in French as fluent as Holmes's mastery of that rigorous and beautiful language the Sultan said, 'Welcome, Messieurs. The air of Stamboul is the sweeter for your presence'.

This was followed by the droll explanation, 'I shall no more declare war on the English language than I would on the English King.'

'And how is London?' the Sultan added affably.

Holmes replied, 'From the point of view of the criminal expert, since the extinction of Professor Moriarty, the most dangerous and capable criminal in Europe, London is a singularly uninteresting city. When Moriarty was in the field, at every breakfast time my gazette presented infinite possibilities.'

I recorded the abominable Moriarty's much-deserved end at the Bernese Reichenbach Falls in *The Adventure of the Final Problem*. For those who have not read my previous annals, I should explain that Professor James Moriarty's criminal network stretched from the Bentinck Street corner of London's Welbeck Street to the Daubensee above the Gemmi Pass in the Swiss Alps. Holmes once described Moriarty without a hint of hyperbole as 'the organizer of half that is evil and nearly all that is undetected in this great city. He is a genius, a philosopher, an abstract thinker.'

'Are you are certain the Arch-criminal is dead?' came the Sultan's query. 'They speak of a resident of Bavaria by the name of Gustav von Seyffertitz who bears a remarkable resemblance. You say you disposed of him down the Reichenbach Falls but perhaps...?'

It was clear the Ruler of the Ottoman Empire maintained an extensive and flattering interest in our cases.

'Moriarty is gone forever, unless you believe in reincarnation,' my companion confirmed.

'Can you oblige me with a description of his end?' asked the Sultan, leaning forward.

Holmes recounted, 'We met at a fearful Alpine place where a torrent pours over a curving precipice into a huge cauldron from whose black depths rises a cloud of vapour. We fought. We tottered together at some eight hundred feet above the cataracts. I escaped his long reach. Moriarty gave a horrible scream. He kicked madly for a few seconds, clawing the air with both hands, gawking over his shoulder at the rushing waters. At his doom. For all his efforts he could not recover his balance.'

'You could have saved him?' the Sultan enquired.

Holmes shrugged.

'Yes, but I had no intention of doing so. The moment I released myself from his grasp I had manipulated my opponent's force against himself to ensure he fell a long way before striking a rock. His mouth opened and shut but his screams were obscured by the roar of the falls. His body bounded off a sharp outcrop, dropped hard on another many feet below, and then another, until at last he splashed into the water, vanquished.'

While Holmes engaged the Sultan's attention so deeply, I was able to take stock of the slight figure before us, the Emperor of The Three Cities of Constantinople, Adrianople and Bursa, and of Damascus and Cairo and an endless list of other townships and islands. Hardly a month went by without his sly, moustachioed face being featured in the latest Punch cartoon. The predominant feature, a great scimitar-shaped nose, shadowed a contemptuous mouth but he was by no means devoid of charm.

At his full height the Ruler of the Ottoman Empire could not have been more than 5 feet 6 inches. His pale forehead was lightly tinged with brown. The decades of constant strain had robbed him of the last vestiges of youth. I estimated he was over sixty years of age. His hair and beard would have been already grey except for the constant ministrations of his thirteenth wife. To comply with the Koranic law forbidding a head of state and its religion to show signs of ageing it was said she plied his hair with a special concoction of coffee, gall-nuts and henna used to dye the tails of horses.

The wildest rumours abounded about him. At the age of 25 Abd-ul-Hamid visited Louis Napoleon at the Tuileries during the final halcyon days of the French Second Empire. Rather than the reality of a short, thickset man in a simple scarlet fez and a plain blue frockcoat, Le Tout-Paris credited him with retinues of elephants and lions led by Kushite slaves laden with golden chains. They said he drove through their ranks from the Gare de Lyon like a Caliph of the Arabian Nights, in a golden carriage drawn by vassal princes, green-turbaned sheikhs and Albanian chieftains gleaming with jewelled yataghans and gold embroidery. It was said Abd-ul-Hamid's shoes were filled with sand from the Marmara Sea so his feet would not be defiled by treading on Christian soil. Alongside the dinner service of solid gold encrusted with precious stones ordered from a Parisian goldsmith, rumour added a crystal chandelier four tons in weight, and solid silver candelabra, each with the mystic number of three hundred and thirty-three. The gossips across the French Capital claimed that on his departure from Paris, the Sultan emptied all the pretty girls from the Variétés for the Imperial Harem, creating a shortage.

I became aware Holmes had stopped talking. He was staring out at the Imperial Garden. A young woman in a velvet jacket and loose entari with an emerald-studded belt stood there, silent and watchful. A rich purple Cat's Eye dangled on a lengthy chain from her neck. Small hands blazed with jewels, diamond rings of great lustre on each of her thumbs. Attached to her long black hair was a large bouquet of jewels made like natural flowers. She held a colourful posy of fresh flowers to her nostrils. Flowers were essential to domestic life in Stamboul. Their sweet smells masked foul body odours and the stench of human excreta. It was clear that satins, velvets, and wools were never washed. Plumbing seemed non-existent, bathing infrequent. At many a spot on our walk through the Palace the stale odour of human sweat assaulted our senses. Even the presence of phenomenally large honey-suckles in full bloom failed to provide a sufficient remedy.

Our host caught our glance.

'Saliha Naciye,' he said, in an affectionate tone. 'My thirteenth wife. With a soul as sweet as blood red jam. She's an Abkhazian. Ah, youth! So impetuous. So…volcanic.'

He turned back to us. 'Saliha Naciye is the most assiduous of all my spies. My day is never complete unless she approaches me with news of some connivance against me.'

I wondered how someone so sequestered, observed night

and day by the ever-watchful 'Lord of the Door', would be able to garner information from the outside world. My expression must have changed slightly. Reading my thoughts, our host exclaimed, 'I agree, Dr. Watson. How she manages to be so well-informed about the outside world is a mystery to us all'.

He turned his gaze toward my companion, 'If you can solve that puzzle, Mr. Holmes, you'd relieve my mind tremendously.'

The Sultan reached inside his coat and pulled *The Return of Sherlock Holmes* from a hidden pocket. He raised it into the air.

'Gentlemen, this arrived before you. Please tell your King his gift is much appreciated. When I lie awake consumed with all my cares, I shall command my Chamberlain to read these cases to me.'

Even while he spoke, the Sultan's eyes continually wandered around the room as if seeking a hidden foe. The slightest sound from outside the room, such as the snap of a dry twig, was enough to make him shy backwards as though it were the crack of a Mauser rifle. His gloved hand darted towards a gold and ivory automatic on the table before falling back once more to his lap.

'Does the Sultan's thirteenth wife take an interest in my friend Watson's tales?' Holmes asked.

The Sultan's face twisted into a smile.

In his excellent French he said, 'She is familiar with one or two but she and the Ikbals prefer Parisian gossip from the

Jardin Mabil or the *Café chantant* and the romances of Paul de Kock—all those grizettes, guinguettes and cabarets.'

He tapped '*The Return*' and said, 'But I assure you, Mr Holmes, Dr Watson's chronicles will be translated into Turkish one by one, and they will be read to me one each night. I shall relate them to her word for word.'

He put the chronicles down.

'I must thank Sir Edward for sending you to my country to enquire into some presumed conspiracy against my throne. Nevertheless, the idea the Sword of Osman can be stolen is quite preposterous, as you will discover when you meet my Chief Armourer Mehmed. His men guard it with their life. I hope you have a very pleasant week here in Stamboul before returning to your country.'

'Your Majesty,' Holmes asked, 'to assist our endeavours I wonder if you could supply us with a plan of this remarkable palace?'

The Sultan replied, 'I can do better than that, Mr. Holmes!'

He gave a signal. Nadir Aga brought over a large album from a side-table. It contained photographs showing the many pavilions and the cultivated gardens and pathways that make up the Yildiz.

'An American visited us. He was an expert on photography from the air,' the Sultan explained. 'He sent a camera skyward aboard a silk-string kite from a ship in the Golden Harbour.'

The Sultan pointed out places of interest including the gate where we were to meet the Head Gardener after our audience, and the Harem garden, the Prince Garden and the Sultan gardens. The American's visit must have been in spring. The pathways were edged with a profusion of crocuses and daffodils. Sycamores, olives and lilacs, limes, elms, hackberries, laurels, the cercis, were picked out in sharp detail.

In addition to the aerial views, photographs of the interior of the Palace had been shot at ground level—exquisite rooms with apple green walls, friezes tender rose in colour, the background of the medallions light blue and lilac or rose.

The Sultan gave another order. The Second Black Eunuch returned carrying the most beautiful object I had yet set eyes on, a gift from fellow Sultan Abdul Aziz of Morocco upon our host's marriage to Saliha Naciye. It was an Adams quarter-plate De Luxe with red-leather covered body and 18 carat gold fittings. 'The most expensively produced hand camera in the world,' the Sultan informed us gleefully. 'It contains 130 ounces of the purest gold. See—each fitting, every screw and plate sheath is hallmarked.'

Observing our host's delight in his photographic apparatus, I was relieved I had asked Shelmerdine to take my precious new camera with him.

The Sultan rose from his throne and beckoned us to observe the fine view over the three seas surrounding the Sarayburnu peninsular. A telescope was brought into the room and erected near the window. We could see the powerful British fleet amid a dozen or more Turkish ironclads dating from the past Century and the swarm of smaller craft. Several miles out I recognised the obsolete *HMS Devastation*. On the principle of the tortoise and the hare she must have plodded on while we engaged in gunnery and torpedo practice during the many sea miles from Gibraltar.

A grandfather clock chimed the hour. The Sultan looked at the hands of the clock and pointed to *HMS Devastation*, remarking 'Her crew has been taken off'.

As he spoke one of *Dreadnought*'s heaviest guns roared. Every window shook. An immense shell soared upwards, dropping down towards the hapless ironclad, hitting the water just beyond her. This was followed a minute later by a simultaneous salvo of three followed by another ranging shot, and a salvo of four separated by 16 seconds. The gunnery crews had got the range. A mighty explosion threw debris and water high into the air. When it settled, *Devastation* was no longer to be seen. To the watching eyes of the world's ambassadors in Pera and the Kaiser's spies aboard the *S.S. Grosser Kurfürst*, it was a deliberate reminder of the length and destructive power of England's arm.

The Sultan pointed at the Dolma Baghchech Palace below.

'I shall purchase several of your 12-inch guns and put them above Yildiz. I moved up here because that palace was within range of the guns of even a third-rate Naval Power.'

An ever-lengthening line of supplicants and diplomats had developed outside the kiosk. We were on the point of being dismissed. The Sultan switched to English, less fluent than his French but perfectly acceptable.

'Mr. Holmes, may I ask how you pointed me out from my look-alikes with such certainty? Both are as identical to me as it's possible for one man to be to another.'

A smile flickered across my comrade's face.

'There were two clues which would have been conspicuous to anyone with even elementary powers of observation. They are so obvious I hardly dare point them out.'

The Sultan's curiosity intensified.

'What were they?' he asked.

Holmes waved at me.

'I'm sure my friend Dr. Watson...'

'Carry on, Holmes,' I said hurriedly, not having the slightest idea.

My comrade pointed at the bejewelled hubbly-bubbly.

'First, sir, your water-pipe.'

The Sultan looked askance.

'But I can assure you, Mr. Holmes, the three were made by the same hands and are absolutely identical.'

'Certainly the crystal bowls and pipes,' Holmes agreed.

'Then what gave me away?' our host pursued.

'The mouthpieces. The mouthpiece you have in your hand is made from amber and set with precious stones, gold and enamels. Only the true Sultan would use it. Perhaps to avoid the spread of consumption your aide-de-camp ordered the imposters to bring their own. They are by no means men of your immense wealth. Theirs were made of simple clay.'

The Sultan laughed. 'Now that you explain it... I promise next time no-one shall catch me so easily. And the second clue?'

'You wear the archer's ring.'

I too had noted the ring on his thumb sparkling in the

late-morning light flooding through the window. Unlike Holmes I had not realised it followed the tradition that even while a Sultan smells a rose he is symbolically ever-prepared for battle.

'I have further advice if you wish to keep your identity secret in any similar test,' Holmes continued.

'And what is that?' the Sultan demanded.

'Cut off your ears and those of the other 'sultans'.'

The Sultan looked shocked.

Holmes continued, 'In London Dr. Watson and I were shown a painting of three remarkably powerful people deep in conversation. One was our late Queen Victoria, another the late French Emperor Napoleon, and the third...'

Our host's face lit up.

'...the third was my father, Sultan Abdul Mejid,' he interjected. 'I know that painting well. I presented it to Her Late Majesty when I visited Balmoral Castle.'

'Then you'll recall in the painting your father was standing sideways on, looking to the observer's right?'

'That's correct,' came the puzzled reply.

I adopted a knowing smile as though privy to Holmes's secret but in reality I was as baffled as our host.

'You will also recall your father wore his fez above his ears...?' Holmes carried on.

'Of course!' the Sultan tittered. 'You would not wear a fez down over the ears.'

'Nor your turban, sir,' Holmes pursued.

'As you say. So?'

'A further question first... you call Sultan Abdul Mejid

your father, by which you mean he was your biological father rather than simply a father to you?'

'He was my natural father, yes,' came the reply.

He paused warily. Then, jokingly, 'Unless you have information to the contrary, Mr. Holmes!'

'I do not, sir.' Holmes smiled. 'Indeed, the opposite. Your ears are identical in almost every respect to those of the sultan in the painting. Through the ear the authenticity of the descent can be clearly observed. I've written two monographs on the subject. We know there are a number of inherited likenesses—eye colour, freckles, the shape of the chin. The shape of the ear is also passed down—whether oval, round, rectangular or triangular, and perhaps length and width.'

Our audience had come to an end. Next we would meet the Head Gardener to discuss plants to take back to England in the pile of Wardian cases.

'I should particularly like you to visit the Star Chalet Kiosk to see Kaiser Wilhelm II's Ceremonial Room,' the Sultan said. 'Much of the furniture was made by my own hands. The Head Gardener will arrange a guide to take you there.'

The Second Black Eunuch closed the door of the Mabeyn Pavilion firmly behind us. With the Sultan's permission to wander unaccompanied, we were by ourselves in the quietude of the Royal Garden, the gaggle of noisy white-fronted geese around our feet. Male and female golden orioles fluttered in the surrounding trees.

I blinked to adjust my eyes to the brilliant overhead sun. Holmes touched my arm.

'Over there, in the shade' he murmured. 'I think she has a request to make. It's clear she wants to avoid prying eyes.'

It was the Sultan's thirteenth wife, Saliha Naciye. Hardly more than the outline of her face was visible, small and delicate.

Her words came in a whisper.

'Might I trouble you to draw a little nearer?'

Wasting no time, she said, 'Today. The Tuesday bazaar. There's a Daughter of Abraham by the name of Chiarezza. She will be wearing a lace-trimmed dress beneath a black çarşaf. You would have no difficulty identifying her.'

'And what should we do when we find her, madam?' Holmes asked in a low voice, both he and I pretending a great interest in the watch-tower on the wooded slopes above Yildiz.

A nosegay was thrust out of the shadows.

'I beg you to give this to Chiarezza with my compliments. She will know who sent it. We women are like song-birds in a cage, seldom able to leave Yildiz, never able to speak to outsiders. Yet, you see,' she added with a sudden tinkle of laugh, 'we like to be remembered by the outside world.'

I reached for the posy. Saliha Naciye paused as though looking around for watchful eyes and added, 'Chiarezza sells trinkets and ribbons and lace to the seraglio. And she tells us news of those scandals which keep us amused in our isolation. Please take every precaution not to be followed. It would be bad for her. She'd be sent away.'

* * *

We came to the Third Gate, our place of rendezvous. The Head Gardener—the Bostanci başi—stood by an ancient granite column in gardens overlooking the Marmara Sea. He was surrounded by empty cages and Wardian boxes awaiting their cargo of birds and rare plants culled from the deserts and mountains of the Turkish Empire. I presented him with my copy of Hooker's *On the Vegetation of the Galapagos Archipelago* and waved an admiring hand at the perfectly-kept formal arrangements of blossoming plants around us. I asked how many men he had at his disposal. He replied 'Two thousand pairs of hands and eyes'.

'Two thousand pairs of hands and eyes!' I repeated in wonder.

He explained the powers of the Bostanci başi extended far beyond the supply of flowers to the rooms. The Head Gardener commanded a corps of the Sultan's bodyguards. His responsibilities included watchmen and guards at the gates and in the grounds, porters, grooms and bargemen. Under his direction, delinquent officials were interrogated and executed.

'I look after the flowers and fruits,' he explained, smiling broadly, 'and it's also my job to prune the court of its bad apples.'

A guard arrived to take us to the Star Chalet Kiosk, the Yıldız Şale Köşkü. The 60-room imperial palace of wood and stone was intended as a residence for visiting royalty and heads of state. Kaiser Wilhelm II's Ceremonial Room was known as the Mother-of-Pearl Salon from the nacre covering much of its surface.

We stepped into yet another wonderland—nine richly decorated rooms with silk carpets on inlaid wood floors, Bohemian crystal chandeliers and Italian marble fireplaces. Here at the heart of the Turkish Empire the style and taste of the last of the Napoleons reigned in the heavy gilt mouldings of the mirror frames and window cornices. Except for ourselves there was no-one else in the entire edifice. The reception room was a vast space with the largest silk Hereke carpet in existence, hand woven by sixty weavers. Shelmerdine told me later that somewhere in its 500 square yards there was one tiny fault, just a knot of white intruding into the ground of another colour, a deliberate mistake to deflect the malice and envy of the Evil Eye—'the emptier of palaces and the filler of graves'—which was otherwise bound to fall on any object of perfection.

With our ceremonial duties over and the horticultural credibility of our mission reinforced, Holmes proposed we deliver the nosegay. We would return in the early evening to view the Sword of Osman. I reflected on the number of watchful pairs of eyes at every part of the Palace. Precisely as the Sultan claimed, it seemed inconceivable a plotter could gain access to the heart of the complex where the magnificent weapon was stored.

* * *

We arrived at the bazaar and sent word of our presence to the Jewess Chiarezza. We were quickly approached by a middle-aged woman. Strong, dark eyebrows shaded hard, bird-like eyes. She was dressed exactly as the Sultan's wife had described, a long loose robe covering her clothing except the sleeves on the lower part of her arm. I explained we were from England and with as gallant a gesture as I could muster handed her the nosegay, whispering its origin. The Jewess took it with a smile of recognition, twisting the posy round and round. Quickly the smile faded. She gave a supernatural shiver. Her hand went to her throat, touching a necklace of beads with the same concentric pattern of dark blue, light blue, white, then again dark blue circles as on the prows of Mediterranean boats in the harbour, safeguarding them from bad luck.

A second later she recovered her poise and broke into a voluble welcome. We were led into the interior as though in triumphal march, past tanks of water and fire-pumps and sellers of mastic and antimony, and shelves of roots, dyes, seeds and sandalwood. Her stall was piled high with richly trimmed opera cloaks, exchanged or purchased second-hand, she told us, from the ladies of the harem. Assuming we were in search of souvenirs for our wives or mistresses, our hostess offered us pins for head ornaments called Titrek or Zenberekli, depicting tulips, roses, violets, birds, butterflies and bees. She pointed at box upon box of tea gowns, slippers and the finest hosiery sent by the Orient Express or brought by steamer from Marseilles.

'This is the latest merchandise from Paris,' she explained. 'French bodices and tight hip-skirts are replacing gauze chemisettes and sagging Turkish trousers in the harems of wealth Turkish signors. Very popular with Englishmen too,' she added coquettishly.

On the other side of the stall, open boxes by the dozen were filled with a dizzying collection of articles of ivory, glass, mother-of-pearl, horn, and metals. Many contained charms against the Evil Eye. A gold ring with masonic device and a watch by Barraud of London had found their way here.

My eye was drawn to a large box filled to the brim with ropes of pearls and rings of every description, some encrusted with precious rubies and emeralds, others with semi-precious carnelian, amethyst and jade.

The Jewess followed my glance. She held out the box.

'How about these for your wives, gentlemen? They are genuine rings discarded by His Imperial Majesty, the Sultan.'

I explained that I was now a widower and the naval commander at my side was wedded more to the oceans of the world than to the better half of humanity.

A solitary ring made of bronze in sharp contrast to the rose-shaped diamond rings caught my attention. I recognised the style from my days in the Far East. The box attached to the bezel could hold perfume or medicines or powdered remains associated with saints. In India such accoutrements were part of the holy relic trade. I wasn't surprised to see it here, in a city known for its religious fervours. To ward off pestilence every second Stambouli wore a waterproof talisman containing the ninety-nine names of God.

I picked through the rings sadly. If my wife Mary had been alive still, I would have purchased eight of the finest, one for each of her fingers. I recall to this day the moment I set eyes on her when she arrived at our Baker Street lodgings to seek Holmes's help over her father's mysterious disappearance. We married in 1887. She was just seven-and-twenty. Seven years later she was dead. I dated events in my life before or after my marriage to her—like BC or AD on the Julian and Gregorian calendars. I still carried her dance card in my pocket, now hardly legible, my initials on every waltz.

Holmes and I were wending our way out of the bazaar when I made a sudden decision. I caught my companion by the arm.

'Do you mind if I keep you waiting a moment? There's something I think I'll purchase from the Jewess.'

Tucked away at my premises in London was a lock of Mary's blonde hair. I would purchase the reliquary ring and put the lock in it and one of the six pearls from a chaplet of the Agra Treasure she left to me in her Will. The ring would become her shrine, in memory of a time, short and ultimately agonising, when I achieved all the happiness a man can hope for on this earth.

'Not at all,' Holmes replied amiably. 'What is it you…?'

But I was on my way.

I arrived to find the stall deserted. The woman who had been standing there only moments before had gone. A man from a nearby stall came over. He indicated he could help, if I wished to purchase something.

I thanked him and looked down at the overflowing box of rings. I fumbled though the layers of jewellery but my search was fruitless. The box-ring was no longer there.

Holmes was waiting for me with an enquiring smile.

'Did you get what you wanted?' he enquired in a companionable manner.

'No,' I replied.

'What had you in mind?' he pursued.

Holmes had many virtues but sentiment was not among them.

I lied, 'Nothing of great importance. The gold watch by Barraud caught my eye. Chiarezza must have sold it the minute we left.'

'Didn't you ask her?'

'No.'

'May I ask why?'

'By the time I got there she had gone.'

Chapter VI
The Sword Of Osman

IT was time to inspect the Sword of Osman. A man wearing a Selimi cap and brocade jacket over velvet trousers and the ubiquitous blue beads at his Adam's Apple was waiting for us. It was Mehmed the Chief Armourer, the Jebeji-bashi. Despite his advancing years the shoulders were burly and the swing of his arm athletic. It was not necessary to study his hands to know he engaged in heavy work.

The Jebeji-bashi led us in silence towards the well-guarded hall where the sword of state was kept between inaugurations. On our way we were shown the copy of the Koran which Osman was reading when he was killed, then a stone cauldron which once belonged to Abraham, followed by a footprint of the Prophet, bottles of Zemzem water, and a handkerchief belonging to Joseph.

The alcove containing the sword was reached through a pair of doors of solid brass, followed by a second pair of iron. Each had formidable hand-forged locks. The Jebeji-bashi bade us halt. We had been warned no 'Ferenghi' would be permitted to approach the sword too close lest his eyes had a desecrating effect. Carefully the Chief Armourer unwrapped the forty silken coverings in which the sword was stored. Suddenly his body stiffened. He turned swiftly. Fear shone in his eyes. His hands clutched the talismanic beads at his throat.

He screamed, 'The *marid*! The sword has been spirited away by the *marid*!'

In a strangulated croak he described the marid, a luminous misshapen demon 'from the beginning of the world…with a soul as distorted as its body', an animated corpse which had begun to stalk the Palace corridors, causing the guards to flee from their posts in terror.

'Go and inform your Master about the sword,' Holmes ordered. 'Tell His Imperial Majesty we shall seek an audience as soon as we have information to pass to him.'

We stared down at the empty wrappings.

Holmes said, 'Well, Watson, we are in the midst of a very remarkable enquiry. An effulgent revenant which steals swords is hardly an everyday occurrence, even in Stamboul. What next?'

'Indeed,' I replied, 'what next?' thinking about the shaken man who had stood before us.

* * *

I awoke early the following morning to a crew member hammering at my cabin door. The Sultan wanted us back at Yildiz. At once. Under threat of torture the Sword's guards had admitted fleeing from their posts in fear when a supernatural being, its body aglow, appeared before them. The panic spread to the Sultan himself. He had immediately dispatched the elegant Imperial caique with its retinue of rowers to collect us. We abandoned our plans to leave the battleship in the relative anonymity of the modest cutter *Haroony.*

Ashore the satin-lined coupé of the deceased Sultan Valide awaited us, the bodywork alive with gold, the curtains closed. Six horses pulled our picturesque equipage up the slope. We clanged along the already-familiar narrow lanes of tinsmiths, candle-makers and sellers of cooked sheep's heads. The driver eschewed the vast public gate by which we had entered Yildiz the first time, choosing instead the second outer gate. Our opulent vehicle eased in incongruously between a line of service carts bringing in lengthy tree logs for the fires.

Inside the Palace walls we were met by the gargantuan figure of the Kizlar Agha, the Chief Black Eunuch. We knew the Kizlar Agha involved himself in almost every palace intrigue and could gain power over the Sultan and many of the viziers, ministers or other court officials. He was dressed in a pelisse of green material with long sleeves nearly reaching the ground, trimmed with sable and other rare furs. Shelmerdine had gone into considerable detail over what he termed the Sultan's 'prime minister'. The eunuch, Head of the Virgins, with the dignity of three tails, controlled the harem and a perfect net of spies in the Black Eunuchs. He led us through the oppressive silence of rooms where no-one dared speak above a soft murmur.

We came into Abd-ul-Hamid's presence. The Kizlar Agha advanced, bending his immense body almost double in loop upon loop of low salaams, like a great bloated sea-monster raising itself from the ocean deep. But it was Abd-ul-Hamid who captured my attention. He crouched in an enormous golden arm-chair. The black eyes fixed themselves upon us with from under their heavy lids with an expression of the most dreadful terror. The pink, filbert-shaped nails of one of the autocrat's hands played nervously with the amber beads of a *tesbieh*. The other hand kept uneasily and restlessly beating up and down, a movement of which I had no doubt he was quite unconscious. The signs of mental distraction convinced me the germ of insanity was seeping out, a trait he and members of his House were reputed to inherit from their ancestor Sultan Ibrahim.

The Sultan sprang to his feet, almost pulling us across to the cascade fountain where the noise of the falling water would cover our conversation from prying ears.

'Now my enemies are closing in,' he blazed. 'Your presence here has unlocked Pandora's box! I should never have agreed to Sir Edward's request. Yesterday the theft of the Sword of Osman—and now more terrible news. My Chief Armourer Mehmed, the man you met yesterday, the finest sword-maker in the Empire, is dead. You presence has caused this—now you must save me from them! The Jebeji-bashi is dead!' he repeated mournfully. 'I shall miss Mehmed. There was not his equal as armourer in the entire world. His swords develop a vampire's hunger. Once drawn, every blade he forged has to draw blood before it can be returned to its scabbard.'

'What was the cause of the Chief Armourer's death?' I asked with professional interest.

'His wife,' our host shrieked. 'He died from his wife.

At the plotters' behest she summoned her husband home to kill him. I've ordered her arrest. She will confess all. The executioners' guild has seventy-seven instruments of torture. Better still, my Chief Black Eunuch has a special punishment for women.'

The Sultan scurried back to the golden arm-chair.

'Remind me,' he called out to Kizlar Agha, 'what do we call it?'

'The Spider.'

'Ah, yes, the Spider,' the Sultan repeated. 'It's an instrument he chains to a wall. Eight red-hot iron claws sink into the woman's breasts. When she's yanked away from the wall, her breasts are ripped off. They stay behind in the claws.'

He giggled.

'—like a spider that's eating its prey, you see!'

He thrust a telegram at me.

'Read!' he commanded with swelling indignation. 'Read!'

The telegram had been dispatched from Greece. Oddly it was in English, the text succinct. It ordered the Sultan to abdicate 'in favour of your son Prince Mehmed Abid or you too will suffer your Chief Armourer's lot'.

It set a deadline, the seventh of September.

I passed the telegram to Holmes who read it silently.

The Sultan's voice rose to a shriek.

'An ultimatum, Messieurs! The whole world speculates on my future. This is proof! Incontrovertible proof! A treasonous plot hatched like murderous hens by those wretched officers garrisoned in Salonika, men I provided with every advantage. I hear the mutinous officers have even selected a villa where I'm to live out the remainder of my days. A villa!'

He thrust his hands into a pile of telegrams at his side.

'Look! Look at these! Despatched from all over my Empire assuring me of my peoples' love and respect. Salonika is not a city! It's populated only by Jews, Greeks, Bulgarians, followers of Shabbetai Zevi, Gipsies. Each of these groups keeps well away from each other as though fearing a contagion.'

Holmes and I stood silent.

'That date, Mr. Holmes,' the Sultan flared, his breathing harsh, 'that date—the date the traitors have chosen—is the thirtieth anniversary of my accession. Telegrams will be received here at Yildiz from every corner of my Empire, even from that city of vipery Salonika, congratulating me on my rule, while this...'—he reached out and snatched the telegram back and shook it savagely—'this orders me to pack or meet my doom on that very same day.'

A sudden piteous look overtook the bravado.

'Their key to success lies in the Sword of Osman. The Sword is their malediction. Unless it's returned within days—nay hours—I shall be caught like a rat in a trap. I'm certain the cooks and scullions and carpenters and electricians—even my gardeners—are preparing to flee.'

Speaking as though the man was not at his side, the Sultan went on, 'Even my Chief Black Eunuch will open the doors of the Palace to the assassins to avoid having the noose placed around his neck.'

'Sir,' I intervened, deeply attentive to Sir Edward Grey's

wish to keep this creature on his throne, 'you seem to know who these conspirators are, where they live, how they communicate. Why haven't you long since accepted the counsel of your advisers—and the admonitions of your thirteenth wife—and rounded up these scallywags? Why haven't you already put them on trial?'

The distraught figure before us cried with some bitterness, 'And perhaps bring about the very events I fear most?'

He made a grotesque attempt at a smile.

'I am like the hen who is asked by the cook, "Dear fowl, would you like to be served up with a sweet sauce or a sour sauce—which do you prefer?" In either case I will be throttled, cooked and eaten.'

His voice dropped to a rasping whisper. 'They plan to kill me just as they killed my uncle, the late Sultan Abdülaziz. They said the Sultan killed himself! At the Old Seraglio. Can you believe it? Why should a sultan kill himself? When the holy men prepared the body for the tomb they saw a tiny mark above the heart. It could only have been the wound of a stiletto.'

Tears welled up in his eyes. 'When I'm murdered they'll put my brother Reshad on the throne as their puppet. He'll do whatever they say.'

He gave us a despairing look.

'Before you sits a man who doesn't know which way to turn. It was my misfortune to come on the stage of history at a time the Empire was bankrupt and could not defend itself against its many enemies. What is life? It's a seed blown hither and thither, sometimes multiplying itself and dying in the act. We reach. We grasp. And what is left in our hands at the end? A shadow. Worse than a shadow—misery. In the face of aggression from without and sabotage from within, I wage as valiant a battle as I can and must, to preserve what remains of this once mighty Empire.'

With a ghastly gesture, as though dangling from a noose, he added, 'You see before you a man who is at present five feet six inches in your measurement. As a boy I prayed to the ninety-nine names of Allah to let me grow up to be five feet nine at least. One should beware what one asks of the All-Compassionate, the All-Merciful. Soon He may grant me my wish. Have you seen the corpses hanging beneath Galata Bridge, how they elongate?'

From his trembling lips came loud, vaporous laughter.

'I ordered my physician to measure the cadavers before and after. A man of my size who dies by the noose lengthens at least three of your inches. My boyhood prayer will come true.'

A slight signal from the Chief Black Eunuch indicated it was time to leave. At the door I glanced back. God's shadow on the Universe, the ruler of vast and mysterious dominions stretching from the Caucasus to the Persian Gulf, the Danube to the Nile, sat sessile, shrivelled, as catatonic as the mummy of Ramses the Second.

The Sultan caught my look. A slight smile flickered briefly around his lips. His melancholy voice followed us out into the garden: 'Dr. Watson, if word comes I'm to be deposed, they will find me reading your chronicles while their tread grows ever nearer. I shall start on *The Return of Sherlock Holmes* tonight.'

In our carriage Holmes declared, as though to himself, 'Dear me! What a rag-bag of singular happenings! I can see only two things for certain at present. The sword goes missing. In Pera the Chief Armourer dies...'

He looked at me. His eyebrows tightened.

'Mehmed meets a violent death during the very hours we know a drama was being enacted in the Palace. Why?'

'Chance, Holmes, surely?' I protested. 'Aren't you reading too much into...'

'You suggest the Chief Armourer's murder so soon after the sword disappeared was mere coincidence? The odds against would be enormous.'

He turned to stare back at Yildiz.

'Clever idea, death, isn't it, Watson?' he mused. 'I wonder who came up with it?'

Back aboard the battleship Holmes and I separated to dress for dinner. As we parted he said, 'We must pay a visit to a cemetery.'

'A cemetery?' I queried, perplexed. 'Any cemetery?'

'The cemetery where the Chief Armourer is to be buried. We need to investigate the circumstances of his death. Our dragoman will have to tell us where and when the funeral is to take place.'

* * *

At dinner my comrade was particularly preoccupied, almost aloof, despite the cheery conversation around the table. The meal came to an end. We lit our pipes. The suggestion was made to play a few agreeable hands of Bull.

'Surgeon Lieutenant Learson,' the Commodore observed from the head of the immense mahogany table, 'one advantage of putting into port here is fresh fruit from the Fethiye market.'

His hands were grasping a large bowl piled high with cherries, apricots, pomegranates, lemons, unripe plums, grapes and figs. He gave the bowl a push towards me. It started on its journey down the polished surface, turning slowly, a carousel of purple, yellow, blue, green and red pennants. I saw Holmes's head jerk forward. He was staring as though hypnotised by the bowl sliding towards us. He flung his napkin on the table and sprang to his feet.

In a voice of thunder my comrade exclaimed, 'Watson, we have been the stupidest fellows in Europe!'

The Commodore and his sea-captains gaped as Holmes strode towards the Wardroom door beckoning me to accompany him. He turned back to address the bewildered company.

'Gentlemen, the Surgeon Lieutenant and I thank you for an excellent repast. We must take our leave. Commodore, would you give orders for an inconspicuous boat to ferry us ashore in the morning?'

Holmes withdrew a page from his pocket and scribbled on it.

'We would appreciate it if you can arrange for this coded signal to be sent at once to our dragoman.'

Outside, Holmes gripped my arm.

'My dear fellow...' I began, embarrassed at our abrupt exit.

I was cut short.

'Watson, the jewellery attached to Saliha Naciye's hair in the garden...'

'Just for that you tore us away from excellent company?' I chided. 'Couldn't this have waited while we played a few hands of...'

He propelled me swiftly across the deck to one of the immense guns, now silent and sinister in the light of the stars, the barrel pointing to the horizon.

'My friend,' came the savage reply, 'do you suppose I would drag you away from your gambling if it was not of the utmost importance? I repeat, the jewels, what flowers did they depict? It's imperative you remember precisely!'

I cast my mind back to the still figure standing outside the window.

I replied, 'To the best of my recollection there were variegated buds, roses, jasmines, and jonquils. And ferns.'

'Excellent, Watson,' Holmes exclaimed. 'And the jewels themselves?'

'If we start at the buds, they were made from saltwater pearls, then the rubies...'

'The colours, Watson, the colours! I believe you have the better of me in colour recall.'

'The pearls...blue, champagne and green. And purple.'

'As you say,' Holmes breathed. 'And the rubies? Again, the colour?'

'Raspberry. And pink. And Pigeon's-blood red. I would guess from Macedonia.'

'You come into your own, Watson!

'Next… jonquils…'

'Yellow, if I'm not mistaken?' Holmes broke in.

'And something orange. I remember thinking it was the colour of a rare topaz. Finally, ferns. From peridots.'

Shelmerdine had told us the Sultan's peridots were sourced from meteorites which plunged into the great Anatolian Desert.

'Peridots. So they were!' Holmes exclaimed.

I looked at him expectantly.

'Surely you noticed?' he pressed on. 'The colours you described in her hair matched exactly in colour and order the garden flowers in the nosegay she held when we first glimpsed her outside the window.'

'I confess I didn't, Holmes,' I responded. 'Even if I had, what should I have made of it?'

'That the jewels in her hair were a gift from the Sultan— they express a message of love. She matches them in the selection of flowers for the nosegay whenever she expects her Lord and Master to notice her—as when we observed her outside the window.'

My brow furrowed.

'Aren't you making rather a meal of it? Given they've been married only two years and she has born him an heir…'

'I make a meal of it for a reason which you might find of some interest,' my comrade retorted icily, 'which is that shortly after we left the Sultan's presence she lay in wait for us with a nosegay to take to the bazaar, isn't that so?'

'She did,' I agreed. 'So?'

'That bouquet, the one she begged us to deliver, naturally you noticed the sequence of flowers was entirely different from the one you've just described. Yet she couldn't have plucked fresh flowers and settled their arrangement in so short a time.'

Flustered, I asked, 'Meaning?'

'Meaning, my friend,' he returned darkly, 'it wasn't just a simple tussie-mussie. She prepared the bouquet ahead of our arrival.'

'For what purpose?'

'To transmit a message. Unknowingly we delivered a secret message. One which may have been pivotal in this matter.'

'A message slipped into the nosegay?' I exclaimed. 'Who'd ever have thought…?'

'…that she'd risk writing a note? No-one. She didn't. Any one of the Palace retinue could have intercepted us before we left Yildiz.'

'If it wasn't a note tucked in the nosegay how else could she have sent it through us?'

'The flowers were the message, how else! It could equally well have been a trug of fruit such as we saw on the Commodore's table. Baron Joseph von Hammer-Purgstall published *Sur Le Langage des Fleurs* over a hundred years ago. He described a secret language known to the Greek and Armenian women with the same access to the harems as the Jewess Chiarezza.'

'Holmes,' I said dismissively, 'even so, the Sultan's wife could merely have been asking for the latest hat from Paris.'

'Then why the urgency?' came the rejoinder. 'Why should she approach two strangers to smuggle a posy out of Yildiz if it concerned only a hat?'

'Then what?' I asked.

Holmes shook his head.

'As yet I've no idea.'

Chapter VII

We Meet The Chief
Armourer's Widow

OUR message to Shelmerdine was met with a swift reply.

'The Chief Armourer is to be buried tomorrow. He'll be interred at the Eyüp Sultan Mosque near the tomb of Abu Ayyub al-Ansari where the Sancak-i Şerif, the banner of the Prophet, is kept. It's on the western reaches of the Golden Horn. Come ashore at 8am.'

The dragoman awaited us a slight distance from the jetty, seated on a cart decorated with high wooden arches hung with thick red woollen tassels. Two large oxen with the lustrous eyes of Brahma the Creator turned to watch us as we approached. Shelmerdine stayed hidden behind the cart's drapes.

'Cover up your uniforms with these,' he ordered.

He threw each of us a pair of trousers known as şalvar and an outer cloak reaching to the ankles, with a cowl and long sleeves. Aboard the cart I saw we were now attired in exactly the same clothing as the dragoman. With a sombre look, he thrust a copy of the *Journal de Constantinople* into my hand. Shelmerdine had pencilled a translation of the headline in the margin. On the front page beneath a large advertisement in English for tinned Nestlé condensed milk ('Protect your baby against cholera') were the dramatic words 'His Majesty's Life in Peril? Who Are These Men? Could they be British Assassins?' followed by 'Skills of a Sherlock Holmes and Dr. Watson of Baker Street Required'.

The centre-piece was a large photograph taken on the morning *Dreadnought* dropped anchor. In the foreground, the Imperial barge was heading towards our battleship. A large arrow superimposed on the photo pointed past the barge to two people in naval uniforms clambering awkwardly into the *Haroony*. We were highlighted by a circle around us.

Shelmerdine handed me a typed translation of the article.

It read, 'Who are these men? They were transported to our shores aboard the great new British battleship. At first sight they appear to be British Naval Officers. They wear the dress uniform of the British Royal Navy. That's obvious to all. But reliable sources tell us discrepancies show them to be imposters. Look at their Ceremonial Swords. See how each sword rests in its scabbard. How can this be? The British Navy officer always *carries* his sword. Our special correspondent checked with the Naval Attaché in Pera. Whenever getting on or off a barge a genuine officer in the Royal Navy would employ the 'Senior Officer's Carry' favoured by members of the British Royal Family.'

I sensed Shelmerdine studying our reactions as I read on.

'Once on our soil these "Naval officers" were observed entering the Yildiz Palace. Why was this pair sneaking their way into the Palace? If they wanted to meet His Imperial

Majesty Abd-ul-Hamid II they could have stayed aboard the battleship. The two men claim they are here to collect rare plants for a botanical garden. If so, why do they return to their battleship each night—why not take rooms where all the English milords stay, at the convenient Hotel d'Angleterre? We must question, are they truly here to pluck examples of the Giant Lobelia to take to Windsor Castle for His Majesty King Edward VII? Or are they 'scouting' the Palace for a convenient spot to carry out an assassination at the orders of the British Government? No doubt the pair has received instruction from the Royal Botanical Gardens at Kew on which of Turkey's 82 poisonous plants they should select for their evil purposes.'

Finally, pointedly, 'This correspondent believes it would take the skills of the London poisons specialist Sherlock Holmes and his medical colleague Dr. Watson to carry out such a "pretty little plot".'

Almost as soon as our feet touched Ottoman soil someone had exposed our identities. There wouldn't be a carter, shop-boy, apprentice tanner collecting dog-dung from the streets or cabman in the whole of Stamboul who didn't know of our presence and believe we were intent on assassination.

I asked, 'If His Imperial Majesty has control over every-thing the newspapers publish, why did he permit this?'

'It was distributed while the Chief Censor was aboard the battleship,' came the reply. 'No doubt someone's knuckles will be rapped.'

A few minutes later the carriage took us over a rise. Ahead I could see a patch of open land filled with grave-slabs.

The high walls were crowded in by the wooden buildings on every side. I looked at Shelmerdine.

'Is that our cemetery?'

He shook his head.

'Beit kvarot – the Jewish cemetery. See how the graves lie feet to the south-east… towards Jerusalem,' he explained.

He stretched an arm towards a small stone hut in a far corner.

'That isn't used much these days but in olden times that's where the corpses were circumcised.'

'Corpses circumcised!' I blurted.

'During the time of the Spanish Inquisition many Jews never got circumcised until they were dead,' Shelmerdine replied, 'in case while they were alive they had to deny their Hebrew origins. That carried on for a very long time.'

* * *

Cemeteries are places where people can linger without gathering suspicion. It would verge on bad manners—an intrusion into another's private deliberations—to pay more than passing attention to anyone else. We felt sufficiently anonymous in the overdress, the monk-like hoods pulled down over our foreheads.

Imperial princes and Ottoman grandees had paid handsomely to make the fashionable part of the cemetery their final home, attracted by the Eyüp Sultan Mosque and its funerary kiosks built by Mehmet the Conqueror. The cheaper graves were located further up the slope or on the periphery.

On the facade of the mosque charming little houses provided refuge to birds, protection from storms, rain, mud and the burning sun. A stand of plane trees reminiscent of Regent's Park shaded the outer courtyard. Their branches supported nests of grey herons. 'Graveyard' cypress trees, some as ancient as the mosque itself, stood as guardians over the silent tombs. Beggars were doing a trade in wax vestas and lemons or a few nails. A small boy with black crape on his sleeve offered narcissi and religious trinkets for sale. Around the mosque several open graves were awaiting occupation.

A man acting as a tourist guide ran his finger along beautiful calligraphy written in white marble letters on a ground of verde antique. 'The first Surah of the Kuran,' Shelmerdine whispered at my enquiry. 'By the calligrapher Yayha Sufi.'

Keeping his voice low Shelmerdine explained the burial ritual. The deceased Mehmed's body was first being washed with scented water at the family home, the ears, nose and mouth stopped with cotton wool.

'It won't be long now,' he assured us.

Headstones leaned in attitudes of gentle abandon, some with replicas of turbans, like old men reflecting. Cemeteries are repositories of stories, remembrances of human beings who have done their time on earth and gone on to the Great Beyond. One headstone inscribed with intricate Ta'lik calligraphy caught my eye. I passed my binoculars and note-book to our interpreter and asked him to translate it. Rather than a Koranic quotation, it was a poem:

'Well did he know the end of this life, for he had been familiar with its beauties; thinking his appointed time yet another gazelle-eyed one, he said "My dark-eyed love" and followed it.'

The combination of hot sun and cemetery took my thoughts back to my military days. Cemeteries in India kept half-a-dozen outlying graves permanently open for contingencies and incidental wear and tear. In the Hills many of these pre-prepared graves were pathetically small, readied for European children arriving weakened from the Plains who succumbed to the effects of the Rains or from pneumonia attributed to ayahs taking them through damp pine-woods after sunset.

Twenty minutes passed. A strikingly handsome wood-pigeon walked busily and bulkily about the sparse grass, its nocturnal home a nearby cherry-tree grown from a mourner's discarded stone. I reached for a handkerchief. Offensive smells from decaying newly-buried corpses were now overpowering the scent from evaporating tree resins.

The sun rose higher in the sky. Swaddled as we were, the temperature was becoming intense.

'They should be here any minute,' Shelmerdine repeated reassuringly.

To pass the time Holmes questioned our guide on the tradition surrounding the Sword of Osman.

'The ceremonial girding of the scimitar takes place between five and fifteen days after a Sultan's accession,' came the explanation. 'After that the Sword returns to its resting place and remains under constant guard until the next Sultan is enthroned.'

'Who has the right to approach it?' my companion enquired.

'The Sharif of Konya perhaps. The Sultan of course. And

the Chief Armourer to check the blade's condition. No-one else.'

'No-one at all?' I persisted.

'No-one,' the dragoman replied.

'Not even the Sultan's wives?' I heard Holmes ask.

'Certainly no woman, however high her rank.'

Just when I wondered if the dragoman had got his cemeteries wrong, a turban hove into sight over the gradient. I pointed it out to Holmes with a surreptitious motion of my handkerchief. The turban rose higher and higher until it was in full view, resting on a body wrapped in a white cloth. The bier supporting the corpse became visible, then the men carrying it. Onlookers seemingly going about their day sprang to the alert, jumping in with offers to support the burden on the final steps to the mosque. I brought the binoculars to bear, hiding them under my capacious hood to reduce the reflection. A short yataghan lay by the turban, sinuous as a swallow's wing. The procession passed along a seated line of scribes clutching pen sharpeners and paper scissors and entered the mosque courtyard. The pall bearers lowered the bier on to a stone while a group of men at a chosen spot among the tombs began digging at the hard ground.

'It's our man,' Shelmerdine muttered in reply to my questing look. 'Hence the weapon on his chest.'

In a muted voice our guide described the funeral ritual.

'When the corpse has been submitted to the soil and the last footsteps of the burial party die away, two Examining Angels from heaven named Munkar and Nekir appear at the sepulchre to interrogate the deceased's soul. They ask three questions: "Who is your God?" "Who is your Prophet?" and "What is your religion?".'

The pit ready, the torso arrayed in a white shroud was lowered into it and turned on its right side to face Mecca. The Imam leant down near the dead man and whispered in his ear the precise replies the deceased should give to the terrible Angels. The mourners threw a few handfuls of soil on the corpse and a large flat stone was lowered over it. A cavity had been carved into the stone, designed to accumulate water for thirsty birds or small animals.

The bearers and mourners dispersed. The three of us were completely alone in the vast burial area. A shudder ran through me, unsettled by the thought of the Examining Angels Munkar and Nekir.

Shelmerdine and I looked at Holmes.

'What now?' I asked.

'We wait,' Holmes replied. 'We may expect the dead man's widow here soon. At the very least she'll want to pray for her husband's soul near his corpse, even at the risk of being captured.'

In the silence peculiar to places inhabited only by the souls of the Dead, I ruminated on my own epitaph. A day or two before the Battle of Maiwand I'd put my papers in order and checked my Last Will and Testament—a small sum to my elder brother, the rest to my regiment. With the pomposity of youth I arranged with the regimental masons for the Urdu words *Sarvatra Izzat O Iqbal*—'Everywhere with Honour and Glory'—to be carved into my headstone. In the event a wound from a flintlock bullet followed by enteric fever at Peshawar would hardly qualify as glorious considering we gave out the base hospital address as 'Café Enterique, Boulevard des Microbes'—and we lost the battle against Ayub Khan's forces. Neither the wound nor the fever did for me.

The words painted on my battered old tin dispatch box— 'John H. Watson, M.D. Late Indian Army'—would be a less over-ripe epitaph, though my attachment to the Berkshires did not strictly constitute the Indian Army. Perhaps I would copy the Spartans -

WATSON
In War

I pondered how my life, like most people's, had seemed led more by kismet than my own will. Perhaps more apt would be *'I only thought to make, I knew not what'* . What I would want buried with me was easier—my watch, whistle, knife, helmet and field-glasses and a memento of my wife Mary's love. And puttees. And possibly one of Holmes's briar pipes for sentiment's sake.

'So what will it be?' Holmes asked me.

'What will what be?' I exclaimed, jolting back to the present.

'The wording of your epitaph?'

'Why, Holmes…'

His hand came up sharply to silence me. He inclined his head in the direction of a stand of cypresses. Precisely as he predicted, a woman had seated herself there, shaded from the harsh sun. She stared in the direction of the newly-dug grave, tears coursing down her cheeks. It could only be our quarry, Mehmed's widow.

Silently the three of us approached her, expressions intent, garbed like a marauding band of Grim Reapers or the Brethren of the Misericordia. She struggled to her feet, staring at us in abject fear as we herded her deeper into the grove for privacy. She mouthed words in Ottoman Turkish which I took to be begging for mercy or a protest of innocence.

Holmes drew back the heavy hood from his face.

'Tell her we're not here to do her harm. We come as intermediaries. We believe we can help her.'

Shelmerdine translated Holmes's words. My comrade's blue eyes showed he was a Ferenghi, a foreigner. The petrified woman's gaze switched to us, half-frightened, half-hopeful.

'Tell her we only wish to know how her husband died,' I ordered.

Hesitantly the Armourer's widow began to talk. An edict had arrived from the Palace. Her husband Mehmed and she were to try for a child. For a boy. Immediately.

'Why should the Palace order that?' I asked.

'They wanted Mehmed to have a son,' came the reply. 'No other Armourer knew his methods. Many times the Palace begged him to pass on the alchemy to another. He always refused, saying he would only pass his secrets to a son, otherwise he would go to his grave with them.'

She threw us a pleading look.

'Mehmed was thirty years my elder. I was his third wife. We had no children. Only girls.'

'The edict you received,' I heard Holmes ask, 'was it from the Sultan himself?'

She hesitated. Holmes assumed his sternest aspect.

'Tell her we are her best hope,' he commanded.

The woman replied in a low voice.

'She says she has no hope,' Shelmerdine translated.

Staring towards the fresh grave, the woman cried piteously, 'They will drown me in the sea. I shall soon join my husband in Jannah—or Jahannam.'

After a long pause she looked back at us.

'The order came through an emissary.'

'Male or female?' asked Holmes.

'A woman. She came to Pera. She said she was acting on orders from the Palace.'

'Was this woman dressed in a lace-trimmed dress beneath a black çarşaf,' Holmes continued.

She looked at him in stupefaction, nodding.

'You see, Watson,' Holmes muttered, 'it was Chiarezza. Her hurry was such she didn't even take time to hide her identity.'

He turned back to the widow.

'Please continue.'

'She said His Imperial Highness was concerned that Mehmed was getting old. The emissary said the Chief Astrologer foretold Allah the Dispenser of Events would smile on us that very night if I summoned my husband. The woman gave me a potion to add to Mehmed's evening meal. She said it was specially prepared by the Chief Pharmacist. The potion would make him strong and I would bear him a son.'

'And you did as you were told?' I asked.

'Of course. I begged Mehmed to come home. Mostly His Majesty keeps him at the Palace.'

'How did you secrete the potion in his food?' Holmes asked.

In the desperate hope these two strangers from another world could help her, the widow removed a small object from her clothing and stretched an open hand towards us. In her palm lay a reliquary ring. I gazed at it dumbfounded.

'Watson,' Holmes said quietly, 'I believe that's what you went back for at the bazaar, rather than the gold watch, isn't that so?'

I took the ring from the woman and examined it.

'It's certainly very similar,' I replied.

'Very similar, yes, but is it identical? Look carefully. We must be certain.'

'Yes,' I affirmed, 'it's identical sure enough. See the scratch on the toadstone. It's the very ring the Jewess showed us.'

'Except,' Holmes went on, 'for one small but critical fact. It is no longer a reliquary ring. Note the hole freshly bored through the bronze. At someone's instruction it has transmogrified into a poison ring in the great tradition of the Borgias. Watson, if you had informed me this ring was missing when you returned to buy it, we may have prevented the Chief Armourer's death.'

I turned back to the unfortunate woman. In as sympathetic a tone as I could muster, I asked, 'And how soon did your husband… pass away… after you administered this potion?'

Shelmerdine translated my question into Turkish. She broke into heavy sobs.

'Hardly had he... I did as I was instructed. I sprinkled it on his favourite dish, okra with cinnamon to deepen the flavours. Then we went to our bed and made love.'

Her shoulders shook with grief.

'I must have sprinkled too much.'

She stumbled and repeated, 'Hardly had he...'

She added something in a whisper to Shelmerdine.

He turned back to us.

'She says just after he carried out his function as a husband things went wrong,' Shelmerdine translated. 'Mehmed sat up and cried out he was dying. He started to complain of pins and needles. His face and limbs went numb.'

A tearful description of the Chief Armourer's final moments followed. Abdominal pain was followed by dizziness, hyperventilation and sweating. As was the custom among the Palace retinue her husband kept an antidote to poison called Tiryak al-Faruq, prepared with painstaking care by the Chief Physician. However the antidote seemed only to intensify his agony and speed his death. Confusion set in. Mehmed no longer recognised his wife or where he was. He died in her arms.

The widow added something in a firmer voice. Our interpreter looked dubious.

'She claims he just had time to make the Shahada, the declaration of faith.'

I tapped the ring over my palm. Tiny specks of a powder fell from the box.

'Monkshood!' Holmes and I proclaimed in unison.

We were familiar with the plant and the poisonous aconite it produced. A considerable part of the attic at our old Baker Street lodgings had been taken over by Holmes's phials of poisons. The array was visited regularly by plain clothes detectives from the Metropolitan Police Criminal Investigation Department, and even the French Sûreté Nationale and America's Pinkerton detectives. Because of the shape of its flowers monkshood is also called Devil's Helmet or Friar's Cap, or more prosaically wolf's bane. It was said Cleopatra used aconite to kill her brother Ptolemy XIV so she could put her son on his throne. The only post-mortem signs are those of asphyxia. The poison's very name in Greek means 'without struggle'.

'Holmes, you and the Sultan were correct,' I said. 'It wasn't a fatal overdose of an aphrodisiac like cantharidin. It was deliberate murder.'

'Directed by whose hand I wonder?' Holmes mused. 'Hardly the Sultan's—and certainly not this woman's.'

With our attention on her the widow gestured towards her husband's now-deserted grave. To my surprise she switched to French.

'Those men, those men who were carrying my husband's body. I have seen some of them before. They were at our house. They came there three nights in a row. I saw their faces, except the man in charge. He always wore a hood over his face.'

She peered up at Shelmerdine.

'Comme lui,' she said. 'Like him.'

Abruptly our interpreter interrupted the distraught woman. In rapid French he said, 'Perhaps Allah will grant you a son from your last coupling with your husband,' adding, 'that is, if you escape with your head intact.'

Holmes intervened. He had an almost hypnotic power of soothing when he wished. He gestured towards the woman.

'Shelmerdine, tell her she has our greatest sympathy. We shall do our best to protect her.'

We turned away. While our interpreter went for a cab Holmes said quietly, 'We must get to work. Otherwise we may be about to let down England's Foreign Secretary, our paymaster, very badly.'

Chapter VIII

We Engage In Smoke And Mirrors

WHILE the cabbie's tired horses stumbled their way along the precipitous streets from the cemetery down towards the shoreline Holmes said nothing. I contented myself with Shelmerdine's conversation. His knowledge of the great city, its history and the ins and outs of the Sultanate was extraordinary and detailed. Now and then I caught my comrade staring at him in a peculiar pensive way.

The dragoman dropped us at the pier. We watched while the carriage rattled away. Holmes swung round to me.

'Remind me, Watson, what is the exact order of our cases in your latest publication, *The Return*?'

There was an urgency in his voice.

I responded, 'First, *The Adventure of the Empty House*.'

'Next?'

'*The Adventure of the Norwood Builder*.'

'Curses!' shouted Holmes. 'Just what I feared. We must make our way back to Yildiz at first light or all is lost.'

My comrade refused to say anything further except 'This is more interesting than it promised to be; quite dramatic, in fact'.

'Yes,' I intervened hopefully, 'it does strike me as being a little out of the common.'

'Ah, then you have an idea who lies behind this little plot?'

His voice sounded surprised.

'Not at all,' I answered. 'Do you?'

'I believe I do,' came the reply. 'I must admit a case which at first seemed simple is rapidly assuming a very different aspect.'

A rating with a message awaited us at the head of the gangplank. Commodore Bacon would welcome us for an apéritif. We were conducted to his cabin. With hardly a greeting Holmes requested, 'Commodore, can you kindly provide us with a launch at first light—and a box of smoke grenades too, if you don't mind?'

* * *

The next day the sun was hardly above the horizon when Holmes gave the signal. I tossed the first grenade into the empty Mother-of-Pearl Salon of the Star Chalet Kiosk. The smoke composition ignited. Clouds capable of blanketing a battleship curled through the vast room and poured from the deep windows. I tossed in a second grenade.

'Yangin!' I yelled.

'More grenades, Watson,' Holmes ordered.

I tossed the remaining grenades in every direction. We began to shout again and again 'Yangin! Yangin!'

Crowds of eunuchs, concubines, ostlers and servant maids came running out of wooden buildings and joined in a general shriek of 'yangin, yangin!' as they ran headlong for open ground downslope. Within thirty seconds the great drums at the top of the watch-towers beat out a warning across the immense palace. Within sixty seconds the rushing figures had gone completely from sight. Not a soul remained. I was on the point of assuming our plan to flush out the culprit had failed when I caught sight of a most extraordinary apparition. A yeti-like figure emerged from the seraglio by some hidden exit. Flames flitted from the creature, magically changing from yellows to oranges. It hastened through rather than away from the gushing smoke. The distinct smell of phosphorescence wafted back to us.

'Holmes,' I exclaimed, 'that's no diabolical intrusion into the affairs of men…!'

'As you say, Watson,' Holmes breathed. 'If I'm not mistaken it's wearing the rubberised ghillie suit we brought as a gift for the Sultan, painted with zinc sulphide phosphor doped with copper-magnesium. Remain silent and observe or our plan is dished!'

The figure hurried on, not once looking back. We chased after it, hurrying along narrow alleyways separating the quarters, through ancient panelled wooden gates and on past bastinado boards and the Abus guns.

We were led to an unexpected spot.

'Of course!' my companion exclaimed, then, unable to contain his excitement, again, 'Of course! The Head Nurse's quarters! Crouch for the moment, Watson!'

With a last furtive backward look, the spectre dashed through the stunted shrubbery of a little garden and into the nursery pavilion. These were the rooms where the bassinets of the Sultan's numerous progeny were put out for an airing. The newborn princesses and the Sehzades—crown princes—would lie swaddled in gemstone-embellished quilts and blankets, their first view of the world a magnificent panorama, the hyacinth blue Bosphorus straight ahead, to the right the sparkling Marmara.

Holmes whispered, 'On the count of five...'

We plunged into an attractive room with fine wall tiling and painted cupboards. Staring back at us like the Damned getting their first glimpse of Hell the Sultan's thirteenth wife, Saliha Naciye, stood with her figure outlined against the flood of light, the still-flickering hood of the ghillie suit flung back, her beautiful features strained by inexpressible fear. Jutting from her quivering fingers was the carved black stone hilt of the Sword of Osman, the blade swaddled in a gemstone quilt. On the bassinet lay a scabbard studded with emeralds, rubies and garnets, the clasps decorated with Arabesque motifs in raised gold filigree.

Every vestige of colour drained from Saliha Naciye's face. Seldom had I seen a plainer confession of guilt upon a human countenance. With a gasped 'Do not be my judge, my enemy', she threw the sword back into the cradle and with amazing celerity swooped between us. I started after her. She dashed down a stone staircase leading into the garden below, like a tigress slipping back into its jungle habitat, unseen until it pounces. Seconds later she was no more than a flickering silhouette between the fish ponds and elegant cypress trees.

'Let her go, Watson,' Holmes called after me. 'We've laid the Palace ghost once and for all.'

Holmes picked up the blade. Far from being simply ornamental it was a well-made, agile fighting weapon capable of cleaving deep cavities into the body.

'Unless I am badly mistaken,' he added, 'the mystery has been solved.'

He held the sword up to the light.

'Or has it!' he called out sharply. 'Is one mystery replacing another?'

His tone was urgent.

'Watson, hand me the dragoman's snapshot of the sword!'

He snatched at the photograph and placed it next to the sword, staring from one to the other through his powerful magnifying glass.

I watched as he turned the blade over. Finally he drew back.

'Take the lens, Watson. Look closely. Tell me what you see.'

'It's the Sword of Osman,' I declared triumphantly. 'Just as in the oil painting. There's no doubt whatso...'

He silenced me with a curt movement of his hand.

'I shall be careful in consulting you on matters of health, Doctor, or you'll prescribe a cure for otalgia instead of kidney stones. Look again at the blade. What do you see etched into it near the cross-guard?'

'The gold filigree flower motif?' I enquired. 'Snarling open-mouthed lions? They are exactly as in the photograph, with rubies for eyes and so on.'

'What else?' Holmes asked.

'The grooves are also the same One, two, three…nine thin grooves. Precisely as in the …'

'Good, Watson, excellent! We're getting somewhere. But at the end of those nine grooves, what do you see?'

'The gold cartouche.'

'Among the gold fronds decorating the cartouche, do you see the names of the first four caliphs?'

'I can see four separate marks in script but whether…'

'So far so good,' my companion butted in. 'They are names to instil sanctity into the blade—Abu Bakh, Umar, Uthman, and Ali. Now look within the cartouche. Come, Watson, we really must hurry! What do you see etched there?'

'Nothing. There's nothing etched inside the cartouche,' I replied.

'Nothing? Isn't there an inscription which, if you could read it, would state *'Assistance from Allah and the victory is close. Bear the glad tidings to the believers, O Muhammad'*?'

I peered back at the cartouche.

'Nothing,' I repeated.

'Neither a second inscription which—again, if you could read the Turkish—says, *'There is no braver young man than Ali and there is no sharper sword but Zulfeqhar'*?'

'Holmes,' I replied, my brow knitting, 'there's absolutely nothing inscribed within the cartouche.'

'And again I ask you…'

I yelled, 'Holmes, how plain must I make myself? Where in the entire universe can 'n-o-t-h-i-n-g' mean 'two inscriptions in Turkish'? I assure you there is no inscription of any sort etched inside the cartouche.'

'Chapeau!' my comrade exclaimed, laughing. 'With you at my side we shall settle this case, if not in the way I believe you anticipate.'

I stared at him.

'How can the fact I see *nothing* help settle a case?'

He passed the photograph to me.

'Watson, my dear friend, take a look. What do you see?'

Incredulously I exclaimed, 'Why, Holmes, this photograph shows there are inscriptions in the cartouche.'

I looked up.

'Someone must have removed them,' I continued. 'But why? Why would Saliha Naciye polish them out? To a Moslem that would be sacrilege. Why would anyone do that?'

'Dear Watson,' Holmes chortled, 'as you imply, the answer is, no-one would. No-one on this earth would steal the Sword of Osman simply to desecrate it!'

'I confess I'm at a loss,' I replied haplessly. 'What does it all mean?'

'The scabbard is genuine but the weapon is a forgery. That's why the inscriptions are missing. They haven't been polished away. They were never there.'

'But Holmes,' I demanded, grappling with this unexpected revelation, 'why would a forger leave out that particular detail?'

'For one reason only,' Holmes replied. 'The plotters had to make their move so fast there was no time for the task to be completed. Something must have triggered panic.'

'What do you suppose it was?' I asked.

'Just as the Sultan suggested,' came the sardonic reply.

'The unexpected arrival of a couple of counterfeit naval botanists, imposters who trip over their swords as they shimmy in and out of a boat.'

'But if it's just a replica, why was Saliha Naciye so terrified when we trapped her with it?'

'There's only one conclusion. She thinks it was the genuine Sword of Osman. She's no idea it's a forgery.'

He looked around the room.

'We're done here, Watson. We too must get out of here before our little ruse is uncovered.'

Smoke still billowed out of the buildings behind us as we hurried out of the monumental main gate along with a hundred other stragglers. Holmes hailed a cab and pointed towards the harbour. At the water's edge I stood nervously watching the tender chugging towards us. Holmes was silent. I could wait no longer. I burst out, 'If Saliha Naciye thought she had the true sword, surely that must mean she was engaged in a plot against the Sultan.'

'Correct, Watson,' came the terse reply.

'For what possible reason could she want to see her husband deposed, worse, assassinated? She has all the…'

'…For the simplest of reasons,' came the rejoinder. 'What comes above riches—above every advantage? What are women most denied? Power! The woman craves personal, palpable power!'

'But through her husband she has…'

'…influence alone. Even so, for how long? I ask you—as Shelmerdine put to us—would you describe Sultan Abd-ul-Hamid as decisive? Is he a second Alexander? A Julius Caesar? Does he wield authority with resolution?'

'Well, no...' I began.

'Is he a ruler who can take a crumbling Empire by the throat and restore it to its former glory?'

'Perhaps not but...' I faltered.

'... a Khan who ruthlessly tracks down and deals with the myriad plots which leap up like salmon in his fractured Empire, not just from Damascus or Salonika or Belgrade but Paris and London too?'

'It's true he dissembles but uneasy lies the head of anyone...'

'...who bears a crown? Uneasy, yes. That's fair enough. Bibbling, absolutely not. In a despot it's tantamount to suicide. It invites—induces—the very aggression he hopes his evasion will dissipate.'

'So Saliha Naciye...'

'She knows only too well the Sultanate is under constant attack yet the indelible mark of her husband is his constant wavering. Two cruisers and a thousand men steaming up the Bosphorus could force the Sultan to flee. See it from her point of view. If any one of the conspiracies succeeds, if the Sultan is assassinated or deposed, Saliha Naciye will lose everything. Her son Crown Prince Mehmed Abid will be suffocated in his bed. She would at best have to flee, forced into living the horrible life of an aristocratic pauper. Every day she hears another plot is in the offing. Every day she takes the news to her husband. She begs him to act. He hears her out. He sits still, not so much a venomous spider immobile though alert to every message travelling along its web but an autarch frozen with fear, a rabbit confronted by a fox, unable to take the plunge, unwilling to order arrests. She decides to pre-empt all future plots by one of her own. She will steal the sword and offer it to whichever conspirators agree to replace her husband with her nine month old son. In one strike she'd become the Sultan Valide, the most powerful woman in the Ottoman Empire.'

An expression of the admiration with which botanists survey a rare and precious bloom spread across Holmes's face.

'How could a woman a mere twenty-four years of age, born in a village a thousand miles from here, come up with such a plan! One must admire her, Watson, and beyond any woman we've ever encountered. Even so, we must present our evidence to the Sultan and the Imperial Divan.'

'But they will find her guilty!'

'No doubt.'

'Then what? What do you suppose they'll do to her?' I asked.

'Take your pick. If she's lucky, a garrotte or strangulation at the hands of the Chief Black Eunuch—or pruned by the Head Gardener.'

I shuddered.

'And if she's not so lucky?'

'Put in a sack and dropped alive at midnight into the Bosphorus.'

My heart palpitated. I thought of the beautiful creature standing quietly in the garden, nosegay to her face. I wondered if I could offer a medical defence and at least ameliorate her likely hideous fate.

'Is there no way we...' I began.

Holmes cocked an eye at me.

'You're hatching some brilliant ruse, Watson?'

'She could plead puerperal insanity,' I replied. 'The sweetest and most harmless of the female sex can quickly develop a hatred towards off-spring or mate at the time of accouchement.'

My voice tailed away. Holmes stared at me sympathetically.

He chuckled.

'Puerperal insanity? My dear sentimental Watson, it never fails to astound me what you are prepared to do for a pretty face! It's a charming but not infrequent characteristic you share with many men. The most winning woman I ever knew was hanged for poisoning three little children for their insurance-money. Puerperal insanity, you suggest! Come, Watson! Does she talk incessantly and wildly about imaginary wrongs done to her? Are you prepared to lie, to put your reputation on the line as a medical man, slur the reputation of the Regiment you served in that capacity, and that of Barts where you took your medical degree? Better you choose *l'illusion des sosies*—that she became convinced her husband was not the bona fide sultan but a substitute who's keeping her real husband imprisoned in a dungeon somewhere.'

I bit at a fingernail.

'No, Watson, you cannot,' my comrade warned. 'Even

now she's in her quarters trying to reconcile herself to the consequence of her ambition. We can only tell the Sultan the truth and the truth alone.'

Almost in veneration he added, 'What a risk she took! In all history you could hardly name half a dozen women who played for such high stakes. Saliha Naciye may prefer the romances of Paul de Kock but the Sultan must once have read *The Hound of the Baskervilles* to her. She appropriated the ghillie suit from the package of gifts to her husband. Chiarezza must have provided the radium paint. A glowing spectre would have unhampered access to every region of the Palace.'

His eyes sparkled.

'One wonders how many other subterfuges and copy-cat crimes your little tales have triggered in our inventive species?'

'And the real sword?' I asked.

'I'd hazard a guess the real Sword of Osman is already in the hands of conspirators. The CUP perhaps. Maybe Prince Sabahedrinne. Who controls these plotters may remain a mystery but I shall make a suggestion to the Sultan which will throw them into disarray.'

I knew better than to ask Holmes to reveal any more at this stage

Chapter IX

Holmes Makes An Unexpected Deduction

HOLMES had always needed seclusion and solitude while he weighed every particle of evidence. After dinner he went straight to his cabin. I too returned to mine. My mind was a jumble. To the gentle rocking of *Dreadnought* at anchor I turned for escape to the opening pages of Clark Russell's *The Mystery of the Ocean Star*.

* * *

A familiar voice said, 'My dear fellow, wake up.'

I opened my eyes. Holmes in his favourite dressing-gown stood in the doorway. *The Mystery of the Ocean Star* lay on the cabin floor at my side.

'What can I do for you, Holmes,' I asked, retrieving the book.

'I'm sorry to wake you at this ungodly hour,' he continued, keeping his voice low, 'but I have a question of the utmost importance. I need your help.'

'Whatever you say, Holmes,' I replied,.

'You recall our meeting with the Chief Armourer's

widow…at the cemetery. Can you remind me at which moment she switched to speaking French?'

I stared at my comrade. In an exasperated tone I said, 'Look, I greatly appreciate your faith in my memory…'

Holmes's hand shot up, silencing me. His expression was grim.

'It's a simple question, my friend. It requires no prologue. I would appreciate a simple answer. The exact wording, if you have it. Then you may return to your dreams, or,' he pointed at the book by my side, 'your tales of daring-do aboard the *Ocean Star*.'

I reached for my notebook and flicked to the pages covering our visit to the cemetery.

'I have it here. She pointed towards her husband's grave and said, 'Those men, those men who were carrying him. I have seen some of them before. They've been at our house. They visited three nights in a row. I saw their faces, except the man in charge. He wore a hood'.'

I lowered the notebook.

'Well done, Watson,' Holmes rejoined. 'I knew I could rely on you, just like the old days. And then?'

'She looked up at Shelmerdine and said 'Comme lui'.'

'You too are sure she said 'Comme *lui*'?'

'As I say, I have her words written here,' I replied, re-opening the notebook.

'Not 'Comme *vous*'?'

I gave him a steely glare.

He asked, 'And then?'

'As I recall, our interpreter addressed her in French with

'Perhaps Allah will grant you a son from your last night with your husband—that is, if you escape with your head intact'.'

"…that is, if you escape with your head intact',' Holmes repeated. 'Yes, he said that, didn't he. Thank you, Watson, that's all I need to think about for the moment.'

I called after him, 'I suppose you're not going to explain why you needed to come past midnight to ask me what the poor woman said in French?'

'Your powers of deduction sharpen with the years!' came the rejoinder through the closing door. And he was gone.

* * *

Shelmerdine forwarded our request for an audience with the Sultan. The response was immediate. Within the hour we were back at Yildiz, bringing the replica sword with us. Once more our dragoman dropped away at the gate.

Abd-ul-Hamid reclined on a couch like the opening scene of a Savoy opera. The Short Magazine Lee Enfield rifle lay against the wall, a box of smokeless cartridges next to it. As soon as the slaves with the censers had once again perfumed the air and made their exit, I handed the Sultan the sword still in its scabbard.

He seized it, thanking us profusely, and looking up at us eagerly, asked, 'Well, Messieurs, have you discovered who stole it, who is plotting against me?'

'We can tell you who took it,' Holmes replied solemnly. 'With Your Highness's permission I will lay an account of the case before you in its due order.'

'Well?'

'It began, as you know, with the rumour the great Sword of Osman would be stolen.'

Holmes paused dramatically.

'The rumour was fulfilled. The Sword was taken,' he added gravely.

The Sultan's coffee-cup halted in mid-air.

In a mix of French and English he said, '*Evidement*, Mr. Holmes, that was the moment even I realised something was up. But I presume by your presence you are going to éclairer everything.'

'The Sword's disappearance posed certain questions,' Holmes continued, unperturbed. 'Who stole the Sword of Osman—and when? And what were their motives in doing so?'

Get on with it, Holmes, I muttered under my breath. Our work is done. Sell the lovely young Saliha Naciye down the river if you must. The sooner we steam away from this monstrous place the better.

The Sultan drew the sword from the scabbard and held it aloft like King Arthur wielding Excalibur.

'My good sir, we know the answer to *when*! The apparition stole it only hours before Mehmed was killed. As to motive it's clear. It was to be used by the plotters to overthrow me, what else? The question is '*who?*'—who stole it!'

'Yes—and no,' Holmes replied enigmatically. 'Yes, there are conspirators intent on using the Sword of Osman to overthrow you but the person we caught with the sword you hold in your hand had another purpose in mind.'

'That being?' came the Sultan's enquiry.

'The intention of safeguarding your throne.'

'Explain.'

'You are the best-guarded sovereign in the world,' my comrade resumed. 'High walls surround you. Every inch of this vast Palace is under supervision. It's an enclosed world, fiercely guarded. Each division has its own commander famous both for his loyalty and zeal. The only passage of entry to the sword was through two consecutive pairs of doors, one brass and one of iron, each with several of the most secure locks. Each night the keys are handed to the Chief Black Eunuch seated beside you. Given the Head Gardener's extra two thousand pairs of eyes, it's impossible for an outsider to remove the sword.'

'So it was someone within Yildiz! An insider!' the Sultan shouted. 'Name him! I shall have him executed. At once. Before sunset. In front of you. You shall denounce him before the Grand Vizier, then my Chief Black Eunuch here will strangle him.'

He paused.

'And eviscerate him.'

He stopped again.

'Better still,' he resumed, 'he'll be humiliated in the streets of my Capital for three days. Then we'll gruesomely hang him and behead him and display his head at the gate where all traitors' heads end up.'

I listened aghast. I felt if I stamped hard, the ground beneath the Palace would burst and we would tumble through into some horrible abyss.

'Then,' he continued triumphantly, as the *piece-de-resist-*

ance struck him, 'we'll fire his severed head from a cannon right over your big ship.'

He made a beckoning movement for Holmes to continue, saying 'But first, we have a saying, 'you shall need to kill your tiger before you arrange where the skin is to be hung up'.'

'In case it makes a difference to the way you kill the person,' Holmes returned, 'the one who removed that sword from its place of rest is not a man.'

A bewildered expression crept across our host's face.

'Not a man? A boy? Not one of my sons, why I shall chop...'

'Not a son, no. Nor any other boy.'

'One of my eunuchs?'

'Not a eunuch, Your Highness.'

The Sultan half-rose to his feet.

'Alors?'

'It was a woman.'

'A woman?' the Sultan exclaimed incredulously, his eyes belying the disbelieving smile. 'What woman?'

Holmes pointed out of the window.

'Saliha Naciye.'

Abd-ul-Hamid's eyes widened. For a moment our host's gaze shifted from Holmes to me. He leant forward to gain a better view of his wife standing in the exquisite garden. Suddenly he clasped his hands to his ribs. He broke into unrestrained laughter. Tears of mirth fell from his eyes.

Holmes joined in the laughter. I had absolutely no idea what Holmes was up to but if the others were guffawing then I would too.

'Excellente! *Excellente*, Monsieur!' the Sultan spluttered. 'You had me convinced the case was solved but I see you're merely joking!'

'I do not joke, Your Highness, not for a moment,' Holmes replied. 'You ask who spirited away the sword you hold in your hand and I tell you it was your thirteenth wife.'

'Explain,' the Sultan ordered.

'Your wife knew of the arrival of Sherlock Holmes and Dr. Watson when it was revealed to the world by a newspaper. When we left Your Sublimity's presence she was waiting for us in the garden. She thrust a posy in our hands as though in welcome.'

'And?'

'The posy contained a coded message. I was able to decipher the code. Dr. Watson and I were to go to the Head Nurse's quarters at an arranged time. We did so. Saliha Naciye was there. A magnificent sword was tucked inside the golden cradle where Your Highness spent the first weeks of life. Logically I jumped to the conclusion your wife must have organised a conspiracy to depose you. I presumed Your Imperial Highness would be replaced on the throne with her son Mehmed Abid. She would make herself Queen Regent, the Sultan Valide, a second Kösem Sultan, the most powerful woman in the Empire.'

'Careful, Holmes,' I muttered.

'But Saliha Naciye is not guilty of treason,' my comrade continued. 'Far from it. Her actions have saved your throne. Dr. Watson and I questioned her. We realised from her testimony she'd taken the latest rumours of a plot against Your

141

Highness very seriously, and that it involved the theft of the Sword of Osman. She had no idea who the conspirators were but they could strike at any moment. She would pre-empt them by taking charge of the sword herself. Her plan was to hide it until the plotters fell back in disarray, unable to get hold of the one symbol of Ottoman authority which could guarantee them success. She took the sword and hid it in the cradle in the Royal Nursery where no man dare go.'

'She told me nothing about this,' the Sultan shouted. 'Why didn't she bring her suspicions to me right at the start?'

'You would accuse her of crying wolf. She feared you'd pay no heed.'

Holmes paused with theatrical effect.

'But when she looked at the sword before placing it in the cradle everything changed. She noticed something strange.'

'Something strange?' the Sultan asked eagerly.

'Something odd about the weapon.'

'Tell me!' our host ordered.

'The gold cartouche.'

'What about it?'

'It contained no inscriptions.'

'Which means what?' the Sultan pursued, frowning. 'I myself have never inspect...'

'It's a forgery.'

'A forgery!'

'The sword you hold, Your Highness, is a forgery,' my comrade repeated. 'Of the most exquisite workmanship, the equal of the original in temper and flexibility. The point of the blade on your finger when you balance it would be within half an inch of the Sword of Osman itself. The real sword had already been stolen. Saliha Naciye realised there was one man in the Palace who must be at the centre of such a web of intrigue. Someone who held a position of great esteem in Your Majesty's eyes.'

For a moment the eyes of the ruler flickered towards his impassive Chief Black Eunuch.

'Someone,' Holmes went on, looking hard at the Sultan, 'who could spirit away the real sword and replace it with a fake. Someone you would not for a moment believe would engage in a plot against your life.'

'Again I ask—demand to know—who is this person?'

'And in turn I ask you!' Holmes parried. 'Any of the ninety jewellery artisans in your service might have crafted the hilt from gold and precious stones but only one swordsmith on God's good earth could wield hammer and tongs to fashion so beautiful a blade. Who could smith such a blade? So malevolent a blade. A skill every swordsmith in Bursa, Damascus and Derbent would give their eye-teeth to possess.'

My comrade repeated, 'Ask yourself, Your Highness, who might that be?'

The Sultan cried out despairingly, 'Only my Chief Armourer. Only Mehmed!'

'Only Mehmed,' my comrade affirmed.

The Sultan remained still for a long time. At last he ordered Holmes to elaborate. I listened in amazement to Holmes's almost entirely fictional account of our discoveries, that Saliha Naciye's suspicions were sparked when the Chief Armourer's wife Zehra came to see her. Zehra told her how strangers had conferred with Mehmed three nights in a row. Zehra feared they were leading her husband astray. The men talked until dawn when they melted away. She was able to catch only one phrase when she brought them refreshments—'The Sword of Osman'. After that she was forbidden further entry.

'Deeply worried for Your Highness's safety, Saliha Naciye worked out a way she could remove the sword until it was safe to return it to its niche.'

'Impossible!' Abd-ul-Hamid exclaimed. 'There she lies to you. The guards would never let a woman get anywhere near it, not even a wife of a Sultan.'

'Impossible for a woman,' Holmes replied, 'but not impossible for a spectral being. If you look for the ghillie suit you will find it missing. If you search your wife's quarters you may find a tin of phosphorous paint. Saliha Naciye hid the sword in the safest place she knew. When it was safe to do so she took out the sword to admire its beauty, the golden dragon-head forming the grip, the hilt, and so on.'

Holmes paused.

'So far so good,' he continued, 'until she noticed the cartouche was blank. It lacked the inscriptions. It was like a beautiful body waiting for its eyes, for a Prometheus to give it the touch of life. Saliha Naciye had seen photographs of the sword from the time of your coronation. This could not be the true Sword of Osman. When the conspirators read of my arrival they must have rushed to remove the true sword earlier than planned. They replaced it with the incomplete blade you hold in your hand. Saliha Naciye asked herself, who could forge a blade of such accuracy and beauty? Only one man. The Chief Armourer himself. Mehmed was in on the plot against you. He had worked cloak-and-dagger on an exact replica to delay a chance discovery of the theft.'

'A forgery?' the Sultan kept repeating, staring at the weapon in his hand.

Amazement and disbelief vied for control of his facial muscles. He turned to look out of the window.

'And *she* detected it?'

'Yes, Your Majesty,' Holmes confirmed. 'A forgery so exact in every detail that without the closest scrutiny anyone could believe it was the Sword of Osman. The final detail could be added within a day, even hours. The plot could be sprung at any moment. Saliha Naciye decided on a desperate course of action. The Armourer should die. That very night.'

'My Chief Armourer Mehmed!' the Sultan repeated sadly. 'And *she* organised his death?' he added disbelievingly.

Holmes nodded.

'The plan was brilliant. She told Zehra she would swear to you Mehmed was only leading the conspirators on, that the Armourer's true intention was discover the full extent of the plot before revealing their names to you. Therefore he would be forgiven. Zehra would be rewarded for her loyalty to His Imperial Highness. But in truth, because Mehmed was complicit in the plot, Saliha Naciye needed his death to stop the conspiracy in its tracks. She set Zehra a condition.'

'A condition?' the Sultan repeated.

'A quid pro quo. Your wife told Zehra to try again for a son—immediately. She must fetch her husband from the

Palace. Zehra was told the Chief Astrologer divined that same night as especially favourable. In time the son would succeed her husband and serve the Sultanate as a great swordsmith. Saliha Naciye supplied a powder, assuring her it was an aphrodisiac.'

'Instead it was…?'

'The deadly poison Monkshood. Which the unsuspecting Zehra sprinkled on her husband's dinner. He died.'

'And the genuine sword, where is it?'

Holmes described how the conspirators infiltrated the mourners at the cemetery.

'There may have been more to their attendance than reverence for the departed,' Holmes replied. 'I suggest you put a guard on the cemetery immediately. Raise the grave-slab. Examine the weapons interred alongside Mehmed's corpse.'

'And if it isn't there?' the Sultan asked anxiously. 'It could mean the end of my….'

'If the sword is not there,' my comrade interrupted, 'commission your finest engraver to etch the sacred inscriptions into the sword in your hand. I have a photograph he can use. From then on you can tell the world only a facsimile has been stolen. The real sword was stored elsewhere. No-one in the world would be able to tell the one sword from the other, not even the Sharif of Konya.'

We took our leave. Outside in the garden my comrade murmured, 'Pity the unfortunate engraver who completes the forger's task. Soon they'll be lighting corpse candles around his grave. Once his work is done the Chief Black Eunuch will silence him forever.'

Our trek to the Palace gates was cut short by a servant calling after us in halting English. The Emperor of all Azerbaijan, of the Maghreb, of the province of Serbia, of all Albania, required a word with Dr. Watson. Would I please return?

I re-entered the room to find the Grand Chamberlain standing at the Sultan's side.

'Dr. Watson, I want to congratulate you on your chronicles,' the Sultan began, pointing at *The Return of Sherlock Holmes* in the Chamberlain's hands. 'One adventure in particular. We came to it last night.'

Pleased, I asked, 'Which case is that?'

'The second one. *The Norwood Builder.*'

My heart began to thump.

'Thank you, Your Sublimity,' I stammered. 'What did you find of particular...?'

The Sultan looked at me with a peculiar expression, but whether one of ire or amusement I couldn't fathom.

'I found one part of singular interest, quite ingenious,' he murmured, signalling the Chamberlain.

The Chamberlain removed the elaborate book-mark and began to read aloud.

"In the outhouse you will find a considerable quantity of straw,' said Holmes. 'I will ask you to carry in two bundles of it. I think it will be of the greatest assistance in producing the witness I require. Thank you very much. I believe you have some matches in your pocket Watson. Now, Mr. Lestrade, I will ask you all to accompany me to the top landing'.'

Silently I mouthed the words as he continued: "As I

have said, there was a broad corridor there, which ran outside three empty bedrooms. At one end of the corridor we were all marshalled by Sherlock Holmes, the constables grinning and Lestrade staring at my friend with amazement, expectation, and derision chasing each other across his features. Holmes stood before us with the air of a conjurer who is performing a trick.

'Would you kindly send one of your constables for two buckets of water? Put the straw on the floor here, free from the wall on either side. Now I think that we are all ready.'

Lestrade's face had begun to grow red and angry. 'I don't know whether you are playing a game with us, Mr. Sherlock Holmes,' said he. 'If you know anything, you can surely say it without all this tomfoolery.'

'I assure you, my good Lestrade, that I have an excellent reason for everything I do. Might I ask you, Watson, to open that window, and then to put a match to the edge of the straw?'

I did so, and driven by the draught a coil of grey smoke swirled down the corridor, while the dry straw crackled and flamed.

'Now we must see if we can find this witness for you, Lestrade. Might I ask you all to join in the cry of 'Fire!'? Now then; one, two, three -'

'Fire!' we all yelled.

'Thank you. I will trouble you once again.'

'Fire!'

'Just once more, gentlemen, and all together.'

'Fire!'

The shout must have rung over Norwood.

It had hardly died away when a door flew open out of what appeared to be solid wall at the end of the corridor. A little, wizened man darted out of it, like a rabbit out of its burrow.

'Capital!' said Holmes, calmly. 'Watson, a bucket of water over the straw. That will do!"

The Chamberlain lowered the book.

"…driven by the draught a coil of grey smoke swirled down the corridor,' the Sultan repeated. "Fire!' we all yelled'.'

The Sultan sighed. 'Wonderful trick. I must try it myself next time I want to flush out my enemies.'

Chapter X

We Pay Chiarezza Another Visit and Say Goodbye To Our Dragoman

HOLMES was standing at the Palace gate next to a line of letter-writers each seated in front of eight to ten little porcelain saucers containing black and red ink. He took my arm impatiently, declaiming, 'We have unfinished business. At the very least we must alert the Jewess.'

Within minutes we were aboard a cab on our way to the Tuesday Bazaar at Salipazari. The approach was lined with row upon row of stalls selling yellow boots bunched together like exotic fruits. On arrival our naval uniforms provided us with anonymity. We blended well with the military uniforms all around us. Stiff-backed Rittmeisters of the Breslau Cuirassiers from the *S.S. Grosser Kurfürst* and what appeared to be the entire British Navy sauntered around in twos and threes, saluting us and each other. Several were purchasing fine embroidered Brusa brocades, damasks, silks, and satins imported by Greeks, Jews and Armenians from Venice and Lyons.

'There she is,' I said.

We walked towards her. On sighting us Chiarezza

pointed at her wares and called out, 'Gentlemen, how can I be of help?'

Her welcoming smile dimmed when she noted Holmes's grim visage.

'Madam, we apprehended the Sultan's thirteenth wife with the sword of state in her possession,' my comrade informed her with deliberate inaccuracy. 'We are here to tell you your life is in great danger.'

Chiarezza paled.

She said, 'I shall start packing my goods. If Saliha Naciye is to die I have no future here. By tonight I shall be gone.'

I intervened.

'Why would you risk your own life to assist the Sultan's wife in a plot against her husband?'

An angry gleam came in her black eyes.

'My people have had ill-usage at the hands of fortune. All we wanted was for the Sultan to sell land in Palestine to the Jews. More than 1200 years ago Sultan Omar prophesised Palestine would be returned to the Jews 'forty-two moons hence'. That time is now.'

She began to empty the trays of rings into a large leather bag.

'It's our land. The land of our forefathers. God has promised it to us. It lies waiting for us. The landscape is empty, great tracts of country untilled, mines almost unworked. There are a few Jewish farmers in the Galilee, along the coast on the Sharon plain and in the Valley of Jezreel. The Arabs live in the hills and the mountains. We wanted the Padishah to sell a portion to a people with no land. Is that too much to ask? We would accept even marshy regions in the Upper Galilee and near Hadera, zones which produce more malaria than crops. Hamid was offered 150 million English pounds in gold. Do you realise how much that is? He says he wants good roads and more schools and ports. He could have paid off his debts with sufficient left over to build ten ports, a hundred good roads, a thousand schools.'

She shot a resentful glance towards the Palace.

'Hamid threw the offer back in our faces. He told us we must forget about establishing a state for the Jews. He said, 'The Sons of Abraham can live anywhere in the Ottoman Empire *except* Palestine'. His exact words were 'Even if you pay me the weight of the earth in gold, I would never agree'. '

'Is that when you asked to see Saliha Naciye?' Holmes responded.

Chiarezza nodded.

'Yildiz is a land where yes can mean no and no can mean yes. I asked her if the Sultan's reply was a yes or a no. She told me Hamid was adamant about Palestine. I asked, woman to woman, how can we get His Imperial Highness to sell us land? She replied it would be impossible while her husband remained ruler of the Ottoman Empire.'

'Was that when she put a proposal to you?' I asked sharply. 'Help her replace the Sultan with her son Mehmed Abid in return for a deal?'

Chiarezza maintained a momentary silence. Then, 'Once Saliha Naciye became Regent a provisional government would immediately grant a charter for Palestine.'

'And your part in the conspiracy?' I persisted.

'First, to guarantee the offer of the 150 million pounds in British gold still stood.'

'And then?' Holmes queried.

'Radium paint.'

'And the reliquary ring?' I asked.

She turned to me. It was clear she had seen the Turkish newspaper revealing our identities.

'Dr. Watson, the request for the ring lay in the arrangement of the posy. I delivered it to Saliha Naciye. It was returned to me with a hole drilled into the box.'

'The box contained a substance?' I asked.

Again she was silent.

'You took the ring to the Chief Armourer's wife?' I prompted.

'Yes. I told her the powder would enable her husband to give her a son.'

She reached for a tray of red apes, black cats, and particoloured cockatoos, amusing mascots for sale to the owners of the touring cars beginning to invade Stamboul's labyrinthine streets.

'Gentlemen, I can give you a good price on these,' she jested as she packed them away. 'There won't be too many landaulets where I'm going.'

We returned to our carriage. I took a last look back. Half-way down the alley-way I could see Chiarezza moving quickly to dismantle the rails of second-hand clothing.

I turned to Holmes, asking, 'Why didn't you reveal the fact the sword Saliha Naciye stole was a forgery? Or that you told the Sultan his wife was trying to protect him by taking the sword? Then Chiarezza wouldn't have to...'

'Chiarezza has a better chance of surviving if she wends her way to Palestine,' Holmes returned. 'I don't suppose for a second the Sultan swallowed my concoction. I invented a plausible story for sparing his wife's life but would that sinister eunuch at his side believe Saliha Naciye acted alone? Even if Abd-ul-Hamid forgives her, he'll send out his spies to search for collaborators. Who supplied the radium paint? The trail will lead directly to the bazaar. It could become an excuse for a night of the long knives against the Hebrews. Chiarezza would suffer the dreadful ministrations of the Spider.'

* * *

The collection of hexagonal bird-cages and the Wardian boxes labelled and filled with plants stood at the ready just inside a Palace gate, awaiting transport to our ship. Holmes asked me to say goodbye to our host on both our parts and set off for Seraglio Point, the brilliants of the Turkish Order of the Medjidie First Class pinned to his breast.

I was taken to a small kiosk. Abd-ul-Hamid greeted me at the door. He was alone except for a pair of identical Angora cats asleep on a costly sable fur. A servant brought sweet tea in tulip-shaped glasses on dainty saucers enamelled in gold and lapis lazuli. A basket piled with plums and apricots sat on a table in the middle of the room, next to summer flowers in tall glasses of water—lavender, pink and white asters and red valerian.

'My dear friend Ferdinand, the Knyaz of Bulgaria, sends

155

me gifts of flowers and fruits three times a week, all the way from Sofia by special carriage on the Orient Express,' the Sultan explained.

Once again I noted the surprisingly deep voice, emanating from so fragile a body.

The Ottoman Sultan added with mild contempt, 'Even in his own country he's known as 'Foxy Ferdinand'. Here, every hubble-bubble café in Pera is infested with his djournals. I know because I've purchased most of the cafés for my own spies.'

With a scornful look he went on, 'Foxy is a subtle and cunning man. He was here in '97, you know, to thank me, his Imperial Suzerain, for recognising him as hereditary prince of Bulgaria.'

He added, 'I admire his talents. But what a flatterer. He calls me 'un Potentate délicieux'. Ferdinand wants Constantinople, you know. He longs for his priests to sing High Mass in Sancta Sophia. His mother has told him his Bourbon blood will take him from a Saxe-Coburg and Gotha to a princeling in the Balkans to the throne of a Holy Roman Emperor. And he believes her. And why not? Her wealth has already catapulted him half-way there.'

He laughed.

'But you must know all this from your time in Sofia, helping the Knyaz to recover the Codex Zographensis. What a yarn you produced from it, Dr. Watson—what a murder! Do the Bulgars really believe in vampires?'

The conversation switched. I was to take an important

message to King Edward. It was too sensitive to put in writing.

'Tell His Majesty that if I retain my throne for a few more years I shall do all in my power to keep my Empire out of the European war the Kaiser is bent on bringing about. However, if an attempt is made by elements of my Third Army to remove me, and they succeed, they will without doubt throw the Empire into the fray on the side of Berlin. If England is ranged against us I caution her to beware the Dardanelles. The Straits will soon be impervious to most forms of attack. My Minister for War has been hard at work. British bravery will not be enough.'

He waved out to sea. 'Even against a hundred monsters like *Dreadnought*.'

It was clear his condition was no longer normal. Once more the black eyes shone with an unnatural brilliance. He beckoned me closer.

'What shadows we are and what shadows we pursue. Dr. Watson, I appreciate the effort Mr. Holmes and you have made on my behalf but if your Foreign Secretary has any sense he'll let the next lot of conspirators succeed! He would release me from my abominable burden. I dream of being unlocked from my chains. Thirty years is enough. I pray only to be left alone, unfettered by such heavy responsibilities. It's certain the plotters will be back. I'll tell them I do not need all my palaces.'

He waved a hand around him.

'A simple kiosk would suffice.'

As though taking the possibility of his overthrow seriously, he calculated on his fingers.

'I could cut down the number of dependents. I would only need half a dozen concubines, a dozen or so eunuchs and perhaps twenty servants. Three or four kadins. And a couple of princes. And,' pointing, 'my angora cats. That would do. I'd be satisfied. I'd be relieved.'

'In that case why doesn't Your Imperial Majesty renounce the throne?' I asked. 'You are rich beyond most men's dreams. You speak several languages. You have a young son, Mehmed Abid. A Regency could be established...'

The Sultan seemed scandalised at the suggestion.

'I fear the consequences for my Empire,' came the answer, his voice shaking with emotion. 'I'm the oak which shades my peoples. You think a wall of iron as solid as the earth itself separates civilization from barbarism, some law of Nature dictates that where-ever civilization impinges upon barbarism, barbarism must give way?'

His eyes strayed to the window.

'If I abdicate they will strip me of everything. Only my name would remain. You are blessed over me in at least one respect, Dr. Watson. When you release your shadow you go to your rest. You are an intermezzo. Like the Salamander, your tail may wriggle for a while, then all is done. Within a century your gravestone will be unreadable. Lichen will rewrite your name and alter the date of your birth and death. In one or two hundred years the passer-by will glance at your gravestone and not know whether you died in 1881 or 1931. A sultan is an *opera seria*. What I do will remain a matter of discussion and examination until the last intake of breath of the Ottoman Empire. According to the philosopher Ibn Khaldun, empires have lifespans like humans. They come and go like periodic comets. Empires are born, grow, reach maturity. Then they decline and die. Your Empire has reached maturity. Your feathers are ruffled only by minor 'isms'— secularism and socialism, suffragism, anti-vivisectionism, spiritualism and vegetarianism. My Empire is on the point of death, like an exploding star. Soon all our pomp will be one with Nineveh and Tyre. Revolutionaries hiding in Salonika are spreading out to propagate their doctrines as far as the barracks of Syria. Even telegraph operators with their eye-shades, Morse-code, and a deep knowledge of my affairs are disloyal to me to a man.'

My host beckoned me to approach him. His hands smelt of costly white eau de toilette.

'Dr. Watson, your chronicles have pushed your comrade to the apex of his profession. You are fidus Achates to his Aeneas. The name of Sherlock Holmes is known all over Europe, all over Russia. All across America. Without you he would hardly have gained the public's attention outside Baker Street. Certainly his name would not be known in every street in Stamboul. Whenever your chronicles are read to me I wonder, 'What if I had chosen my fate?' What if I hadn't become a Sultan, what would I most wish I had been?'

'And the answer?'

'The world's greatest consulting detective, no less.'

I turned to go. The Sultan's deep voice restrained me.

'Dr. Watson, before you leave I want you to accept a memento of your visit.'

He leaned over the edge of the sofa and pulled an ornate chest to the fore. At the touch of a hidden lever the lid sprang open to reveal a treasure of jewels, emerald necklaces and flower brooches made of exquisite blue and white diamonds. Rich purple of the amethyst vied for the sunlight with the gentler fire of rubies, deep-red sapphires and hundreds, perhaps thousands of flawless diamonds—maroon, green, deep blue, cushion-shaped from the Golconda mines of India, as wondrous as those I set eyes on once a long time before, at the Court of Sher Ali Khan.

'In happy remembrance of your visit to my country I beg you to dip your hands into this chest,' came the Sultan's beguiling voice. 'Take whatever you can grasp! I know your pen is influential all over the world. I am represented abroad as a despotic and cruel ruler. I'm certain you will write of me kindly, even if the Turkish historians discredit my reputation. I beg you to put my rule to the Western world in the proper light.'

I cast around for diplomatic words to escape my deep embarrassment.

'Your Majesty,' I stammered, 'I cannot possibly accept such a... Why... Sir Edward would absolutely forbid me to...'

The Sultan's hand rose abruptly. He kicked the lid of the box shut and reached inside his coat.

'Then you must not refuse this gift,' he continued, 'or (at which he gave a loud laugh)...or you will insult me. Then the Commodore might have to fish you out of the Marmara Sea!'

Still chuckling, he withdrew the gold and ivory automatic.

He went on, 'I understand you have a fine collection of such weapons. The Prince Regnant of Bulgaria gave you a Philadelphia Baby Derringer, did he not?'

Tapping me playfully on the arm, he continued, 'No doubt Foxy told you it was the very pistol John Wilkes Booth used in his assassination of President Abraham Lincoln on the night of April 14, 1865?'

'Yes, that is certainly what he told me.'

'He gave me one too!' responded the Sultan, 'telling me the same story.'

We broke into helpless guffaws.

'Dr. Watson,' he resumed, handing the pistol to me, 'you must not refuse me. *This* pistol deserves a good home. It's caused the death of at least five would-be assassins by my very own hand. It could be useful to you one day too.'

Shelmerdine's description of Abd-ul-Hamid's enthusiasm for lawnmowers, cigarette lighters and musical boxes flashed into my mind. I replied, 'Your Highness, I shall accept your gracious gift on one condition, that on behalf of Sherlock Holmes, England and myself, you will accept these very powerful Ross military binoculars.'

I grabbed the pair of prismatic binoculars from around my neck and held them out.

I had scrambled out of an awkward place. The Sultan's eyes lit up. With an expression of appreciation he grasped the strap and pulled it over his head.

Our exchange of gifts completed, my host clambered to

his feet. As he led me towards the doorway he pointed at the remarkable pistol now in my pocket.

'I absolutely hate putting anyone to death but it is important that a ruler does so once in a while.'

The thought clearly cheered him. He wiggled a forefinger.

'Therefore,' he continued, 'every once in a while my trigger-finger gets itchy.'

His expression changed. He pressed my arm in a cold, dank grasp.

'When you return to England, please give my good wishes to the King. Our paths intersect in many ways. He may rule over more than 50 million Muhammadans in India but I am their spiritual overlord. Tell him I want to deepen my friendship with England. England asks nothing of me and I have nothing to fear of her.'

Given the implied threat to encourage our Indian subjects to revolt, I asked, did the Sultan mean a cordial exchange of letters or a fully-fledged agreement such as the King had signed with France two years before?

'An Entente!' he exclaimed, his eyes lighting up. 'Yes. Certainly. That would be good. An Entente Cordiale.'

He reflected for a moment.

'Though perhaps not quite such an open one. More discreet. More surreptitious. We could get Foxy Ferdinand to word it. He's a master of the *politique de bascule*.'

There was another pause, then, 'Dr. Watson, it would benefit me greatly if England signed such an agreement. I could fend off the Young Turks with all their slavish admiration of the Kaiser.'

A crafty expression was drifting across the Sultan's face. Unaware Sir Edward Grey was well apprised of his pact with the Kaiser he continued, 'We could sign a secret military convention, a secret annexe. Guarantee the integrity of our territories if either of us is attacked. You will tell His Imperial Majesty what we have discussed?' he asked eagerly.

'The very next time I see him,' I promised.

It was clear he and the Bulgarian Knyaz had much in common. Both would coquette first with one and then another of the Powers as they deemed best for the advancement of their interests, and as quickly double-cross the one or other.

Abd-ul-Hamid face brightened.

'Dr. Watson, one more thing. Please thank Mr. Sherlock Holmes for the lecture on ears. How their shape is passed down father to son.'

'What of it?' I asked, mystified.

'It has proved of quite inestimable value. Last night I conducted a survey of my fourteen sons. Four had ears they couldn't possibly have inherited from me.'

With a ghastly grin he added, 'At midnight my Head Gardener did a bit of weeding out.' He pointed out at the glistening Bosphorus, calm and beautiful in the summer sun. 'Their mothers too.'

Our association had come to its end. There was no photograph to mark the occasion, no formal finish. There was no vote of thanks, no valedictory speech. We just left off meeting. The dog barks, the caravan moves on.

The air was heavy with the scent of jasmine as I walked

through the gardens of this Eastern palace for the last time. Bulbuls sang in the hedges and trees. With relief I emerged well before dusk set in. No other comparable space on earth could be as brooding and baleful even by day.

Holmes was waiting for me at an agreed rendezvous on Seraglio Point. From the heights we had a most excellent view to the shores of Scutari over the Sweet Waters, the Bosphorus, the Sea of Marmara and its islands. I gave an amusing account of how I had presented my binoculars to the 'Padishah' before spending a short while bringing my notes up to date. I copied down the words of an earlier English traveller to these parts, Lady Mary Wortley Montagu: 'From where we stood, the faraway minarets of the city mingled with sea and shore, light and shade. The reds of the sunset were dissolving into greys. The softness and the Eastern charm could hardly be equalled anywhere else in the whole world'.

* * *

It was nearing the time to go to the water's edge to await the arrival of the cases and cages and shake Stamboul's dust and dung from our shoes. We engaged a Spider phaeton drawn by two smart snowy-coated stallions to take us down the steep slope to the Golden Horn. *Dreadnought* was dressed all over with flags. An anchor was suspended from the starboard deck edge. Her funnel covers had been removed. Steam billowed up. On Galata Bridge, gaggles of fishermen were trying their luck. Ever impatient, Holmes went ahead to the battleship. I stood alone at the dockside waiting for the birds and plants, reeling from the revelation he had made only moments earlier.

'How is it possible?' I asked myself.

Holmes had sworn me to complete secrecy.

'If you reveal what I've just told you to anyone—anyone at all,' he adjured, 'you'll have broken the great trust between us, and the honour of your regiment in India—the Bombay Grenadiers, wasn't it?'

'No, Holmes, it wasn't,' I retorted coldly. 'The Fifth Northumberland Fusiliers, then the Berkshires.'

Ignoring my rebuke he insisted on an embargo on the information he had just imparted. I assented reluctantly.

'Nevertheless Holmes, I find it impossible to believe what you say. I'm perfectly certain the air of Stamboul has got to you. You're suffering from some unaccountable hallucination, what you called *l'illusion des sosies.*'

'I'll agree with you, my friend,' he replied, 'if when he turns up his sole topic of conversation is England's weather.'

With that, Holmes stepped aboard the *Haroony* and chugged away.

* * *

Minutes later a timber-jam came down the slope, the motion akin to a ship in heavy seas, alarmingly tip-tilting to the verge of upsetting. The cart overflowed with Wardian cases filled with plants selected by the Sultan's Head Gardener and cages choc-a-bloc with flurried birds destined for the Zoological Society. Some birds I recognised from my stint in Afghanistan—woodpeckers, rails and crakes, black storks, Glossy Ibises and a pair of Greater Flamingos.

165

Behind it hurried our dragoman, my Quarter Plate camera under one arm, some packages in his free hand. On sighting me at the waterside a frown was replaced by his eager half-smile. He handed over the camera and the packages of saffron and Kofte Bahari. We stood talking while the cases and cages were swung from the land into *Dreadnought*'s launch. I'd grown to like Shelmerdine in our short time together. I did not share Holmes's unaccountable coolness, even deprecation towards him. Our interpreter had performed his task impeccably. His interpretation of language and culture was greatly enhanced by his knowledge of English customs, as displayed in, 'If you meet Djafer Aga, take care. Don't be fooled by your English concept of a eunuch. The First Black Eunuch is the third highest-ranking officer of the empire, after the Sultan and Ali Pasha, the Grand Vizier. He's the equivalent of your erstwhile Grooms of the Stole'. Noting the smart naval uniforms at our first encounter he exclaimed (disingenuously, I realised later), 'Mr. Holmes, a Royal Navy Commander! Dr. Watson, an RN Surgeon Lieutenant! I was expecting two middle-aged gentlemen sporting tweed suits, black silk cravats, bowler hats and Javanese canes'.

I pointed up at the Palace.

'The Chief Armourer's body,' I asked. 'What will happen to it? Will they...?'

Perhaps because we were parting for the last time he replied in a more unceremonious manner: 'Terrible things, Doctor! After your revelations they'll disinter his corpse from the boneyard and string his *disjecta membra* on pegs at the outside gate.'

166

'Really!' I exclaimed, revolted.

Shelmerdine grinned.

'No, though you might expect that. In fact he'll be treated with great respect. The Padishah himself intends to chance his own life and attend a special ceremony at the grave-side...weeping.'

Startled, I asked, 'Why would the Sultan...?'

'Think of it, Dr. Watson, do you suppose Abd-ul-Hamid will want his people to know someone so close to him, so beholden to him, would throw his lot in with conspirators intent on sending the Great Khan packing—the Custodian of the holy sites of Makkah, Madinah and Jerusalem menaced by a plot at whose core lay his own bladesmith? For the same reason he'll go along with Mr. Holmes's ingenious exculpation of Saliha Naciye without believing a tittle of it. The Sultan knows the Chief Armourer could have replaced the Sword of Osman with a Prussian cavalryman's rusty sabre from the Battle of Waterloo and she wouldn't know the difference. She'll survive only because it makes a much more favourable story to put around the bazaars that a plot by renegades to dethrone him was *foiled* rather than led by the mother of his son. You may be certain that Saliha Naciye will find her freedoms curtailed. There'll be no further passage of nosegays between the seraglio and the bazaars.'

'Will you report Mehmed's death in the newspapers?'

'Certainly,' he affirmed.

'That he died of...?'

'Gout.'

I reflected how Holmes and I had merely to make our

way in the country of our birth, a land where the rule of law was preeminent, where justice could be obtained and a normal life led not just day to day but from conception to burial. By contrast, daily—hourly—Shelmerdine had to observe rules of etiquette as overblown and intricate as the Moghul. He had to survive a despotism where talk even in one's kitchen was dangerous, to wend his way in a world of the utmost cruelty and unpredictability. Where life was so dispensable a sultan could drown his entire harem in a fit of jealousy and rage.

Shelmerdine dropped his voice. 'Doctor, I hope I've been of some help in your endeavours…you said there was a second plot. The schemers must fear imminent exposure. As you and Mr. Holmes may never grace our shores again, kindly tell me—in the utmost confidence—what about this other conspiracy?'

I looked up at Yildiz. In my mind I could see the rose and tulip and fenugreek gardens, the bowers with ivy and wisterias, the lion statues, water pouring from their mouths, in whose proximity you could talk confidentially. Here too, at the water's edge, we could talk in safety, our voices drowned by the constant roar of harbour traffic and the shouts of people selling their wares on Galata Bridge.

I answered, 'The moment we recognised a forgery it was clear there was a second plot, organised with great care and brilliance. One which was at the very instant of being sprung. The real sword had already been stolen—but by whom? Had we not arrived when we did, I'm confident the conspiracy would have succeeded. The Sultan would be in exile. Or dead.'

'Yet you have no clues at all to the malefactors' identities?'

'Regarding the head conspirator, no. Nothing,' I replied. 'Unfortunately, when Saliha Naciye poisoned the Chief Armourer, she killed off the trail. However my comrade has deduced the identity of the principal agent.'

'The principal agent!' Shelmerdine exclaimed.

His eyes, unblinking, were fixed on mine.

'The mastermind's agent,' I affirmed. 'You see, there was one critical difference between the plots.'

'Which was?'

'One conspiracy could only have been conducted from *within* the Palace. That was clearly Saliha Naciye's.'

'And the other?'

'By a collaborator quartered outside the walls of Yildiz.'

'Why certainly, we know the Young Turks...'

'Nowhere near as far off as Salonika,' I replied.

'Then where?'

'In the very heart of Stamboul.'

Shelmerdine looked shocked. After a short while he asked, 'You say Mr. Holmes has worked out that villain's identity?'

'He has.'

'If that's so,' Shelmerdine responded, 'why doesn't your colleague reveal his name to the Sultan?'

He gestured towards the Bosphorus. 'So His Sublimity can wreak his customary revenge.'

'Because the agent may well know where the true Sword of Osman lies concealed,' I replied.

'And that could be of value to you?'

'To Holmes and me personally, no. To a certain Imperial Power, yes.'

The dragoman cast a speculative eye at *HMS Dreadnought*.

'That Power being?'

'One which doesn't for the while seek the collapse of the Ottoman Empire.'

'Ah,' he said.

After a pause he asked, 'By any chance would it be England?'

'It's possible.'

Shelmerdine laughed loudly as though relieved.

'I can see your hands are tied,' he continued. 'But you say you know who he is, by name even?'

'We shall never reveal the surrogate's identity, certainly not to Yildiz.'

Shelmerdine held out his hand in a final goodbye. With a comical pomposity of manner he bowed solemnly.

'It's been,' he said, 'one of the great privileges of my life to have met you in person.'

Whether he meant Holmes and me or, flatteringly, me alone, I couldn't tell.

As he turned to leave he remarked with uncommon familiarity, 'Dr. Watson, I admire loyalty to one's friends but I put it to you, Mr. Sherlock Holmes hasn't the faintest idea who this agent is, any more than he can identify the mastermind. The great gumshoe bluffs.'

The impudent use of 'gumshoe' riled me. When he had

taken a few paces I called out, 'The great gumshoe never bluffs, Shelmerdine'.

I pointed up at the Palace glinting in the evening sun. 'But don't worry, the skeleton in your closet is perfectly safe with us.'

I stepped on to the loaded pinnace and debouched. Because of the dragoman's unaccustomed effrontery I had broken the solemn vow wrung from me by Holmes barely thirty minutes earlier. Shelmerdine stood alone among the hustle and bustle of the shore. He called out something, his words indistinguishable in the hubbub of evening traffic and the whistling of boats.

* * *

Early the next morning a steamboat passed close to our battleship. A small package addressed 'to the Surgeon Lieutenant' was thrown up to a watchful crew member. I opened the parcel to discover a stonepast dish from the Iznik potteries. A beautiful bird, blue, champagne and green, rested on gently swaying plants bearing pinkish-purple carnations, yellow tulips, and cyan hyacinths. There was no note. The colours of the dish's flowers echoed the nosegay Saliha Naciye held to her nostrils when we first caught sight of her through the pavilion window. The Sultan's thirteenth wife had already devised a new line of communication to the outside world.

Led by *Dreadnought* the fleet steamed into the Sea of Marmara on its journey back to Gibraltar. Within minutes we attained full speed. I watched the minarets and domes of the ancient city fast disappearing behind us. As with Alice returning from Wonderland, 'all would change to dull reality'.

171

The curtain of a past which had swung aside only days before was swinging shut. The brilliance of Yildiz, the kiosks and rooms—the gardens—all would evanesce. The Sultan, the Chief and Second Black Eunuchs, the dead Chief Armourer, the exiled Chiarezza, Saliha Naciye herself, in or out of the luminous ghillie suit, Stamboul and its smells and bazaars and spies and yelps of stray dogs, would tip-toe away to a dark place, like the genii of *One Thousand And One Nights*. It would only be through access to my notes that I would recollect reality from myth.

The British fleet came alive with lights, flags and semaphore, at pains to show the Navy as competent and ready for action. *Dreadnought*'s heavy guns thundered. The detonations would make all Stamboul's hermetically latticed windows shake. It was a convincing adieu, a demonstration of England's ability to 'hit first, hit hard and go on hitting' anywhere in the world. About seven sea miles out we heard a single cannon shot from the direction of the General Staff Headquarters in Tophane. I looked at my pocket watch. It was around a quarter past nine, the customary time for the cannon to announce the death of a traitor.

* * *

Eight days after we steamed away from Galata Bridge Gibraltar loomed. For the final stage of the journey I assisted the battleship's regular naval surgeon in treatment of the pox from which it seemed half the crew now suffered. On the last night at sea Holmes presented Commander Bacon with a precious First Edition of *The Washing Away of Wrongs*, composed in 1235 A.D. by the Chinese death investigator

Sung Tz'u. In return the Commander presented us with the fruit bowl which had set Holmes on Saliha Naciye's trail, now filled with the finest dates, almonds, dried apricots, topped with Rahat loukoum from Hadji Bekir's Lumps of Delight factory near the Galata Bridge head.

At sun-up I packed my belongings and left them at the open cabin door. A rating hurried out from the electric telegraph booth. He stopped when he saw me and held out a sealed envelope.

'Lieutenant Learson, sir, if you're on your way to join Commander Hewitt, could I ask you to hand this to him? It came this morning.'

He paused.

'And, sir, any chance you could leave *The Mystery of the Ocean Star* behind when you go?'

I gave Holmes the message. He read it and passed it across to me without comment.

'Sir Edward Grey to Mr. Sherlock Holmes.
BALMORAL CASTLE
August 3, 1906.

'My dear Holmes, I have discussed with the King in private your latest endeavours on our country's behalf. You have not only his deepest thanks and those of His Majesty's Government (even though neither's gratitude cannot be openly displayed) but those of His Imperial Majesty, the Sultan, who professes to be '*touché jusqu'aux larmes*' by your kindness and concern. Critics may find many mistakes and short-comings in England's foreign policy of the last hundred years but it is at least a tenable view that in this instance the conduct of those affairs has been suited to the development and needs of our Empire.

'Last week I gathered my courage and returned to "the tin house". I could not get away from the Foreign Office until the last train and arrived about midnight, after a moonlight drive from Winchester, thinking all the way about the walk with Dorothy along the same road at the same time of night. The following day was filled with her presence beside me, here and there some place or tree lit, as I looked, by a happy memory, like a gleam of light falling on it.'

I read the next sentence and lowered the page. Tears sprang to my eyes. Grey was expressing exactly how I felt about my own dear, dead wife. He wrote, 'Her life was like a soft white cloud which came out of nothing into a summery, hazy heaven and as softly disappeared'. Those words would have been entirely appropriate etched on Mary's stone in the tiny Brightling cemetery, adjacent to the church where we were married, in whose nearby wooded valleys we spent our honeymoon. In the event the mason carved the exquisite line from *The Rubaiyat*—'The Bird of Time has but a little way/ To fly...'

I returned to Grey's letter.

'The Saturday after your feet touch England's soil once more, I hope you and Dr. Watson will accept an invitation to lunch at Chequers Court, the home of the Clutterbucks at the foot of the Chiltern Hills. I plan to be there. The oak-roofed hall is said to date to the time of King John, a remnant of a former house. It has its own ghost, of course. The Clutterbucks will introduce us to more recent, more tangible residents—an eider duck, a tufted duck, a red-headed pochard, two wigeons, and an elderly Shoveler duck. The Shoveler dines at table with the family, on special food.

'I have heard you are inclined to refuse honours created by Man. I hope you will accept one from the great Deity who commands our fate. We shall plant a tree on the East Lawn, a specimen of *Quercus ithaburensis macrolepsis*, one of the valonia oaks returning with you from the Dardanelles. For centuries the Sherlock Holmes tree will flourish in the grounds of Chequers in abiding recognition of the many services you have performed for our country.

'May I count on—and look forward to—your visit?

'*L'un de vos fervents.*

'E. Grey'

Chapter XI

A Most Surprising Letter Arrives From Mycroft

AT Chequers on the Saturday a further communication arrived, addressed to Sherlock Holmes. It was deeply scored in red ink and marked 'Most Secret'. We were clustered in the grounds with Sir Edward Grey and the Clutterbucks, having planted the commemorative Valonia on Coombe Hill. The sapling stood next to an ancient clump of chequer trees after which the house was named. Holmes squinted at the pages of foolscap and handed them to me. I excused myself and moved away from our hosts.

The letter was from Mycroft, penned in duck-egg green ink. It was one of the most stupefying documents I have ever read.

'My dear Sherlock, I must immediately thank you for returning with a good supply of saffron and allspice and am pleased to welcome you back intact. By now you will have deduced that my views on matters Ottoman differ in kind from Edward Grey's more absolutely than I could ever describe in words. He may be standing next to you as you read this but I do not hold it uncharitable of me to say the Foreign Secretary lacks every skill a diplomat requires, social brilliance, the smiling falsehoods, the cunning to move gracefully among traps and mines, the ruthless outlook.

You solved the riddle of the Sword(s) of Osman in short order. In doing so, I hold you have, single-handedly, made a great war in Europe inevitable. If the British Government should have had the intention to embroil the political situation and lead towards a violent explosion, they could not have chosen a better means than to send you to Constantinople. You and I came up against each other for the first time, and you came out in front.

I do not absolve myself from a charge of deviousness. I knew the Sword of Osman had been shanghaied before your arrival. I hoped the Sultan would awaken from his torpor and eradicate his most dangerous enemy, the Young Turks and their Committee of Union and Progress, root and branch. A badly weakened CUP could ensure the sultanate would fall instead to their rival, Prince Sabahedrinne. It was my calculation and those of other members of the Diogenes Club (several of whom sit in the Cabinet alongside Grey) that precisely because the Prince fully intends to implement reforms and espouses liberal principles the edifice of a fractious Empire would collapse—on the proven principle of give an inch and an invigorated populace will take a mile. Within months, like Russia's reformist Tsar Alexander, Sabahedrinne would in turn be assassinated.'

'So that's what they really get up to at the Diogenes,' I breathed.

Mycroft continued, 'As with Bloody Sunday in St. Petersburg last year, economic paralysis and disorder would incite large-scale political demonstrations. The Ottoman Empire would shatter. The chaos would open up access to untold quantities of oil and once-in-a-half-millennium pickings in the Near East for the Empires of Europe. Germans, Arabs, Kurds, Russians, Armenians, French, Greeks, Turks, Bulgarians, Italians and Israelites would fight for the scraps. There would be rich spoils for the French in Lebanon and Syria, for the Italians in Libya and the Dodecanese islands. Britain would take effective control of the lower Red Sea littoral and the island of Tiran, the only good anchorage in the Gulf of Akaba. The last vulnerabilities on our routes to the Far East would thus be closed, and with Abd-ul-Hamid's departure his fiddling among the Mussulmen of British India too.
'The Prussian mischief-makers will allow Grey to keep the peace only as long as it suits them. They hunger for a full share of the mastery of the world. Far from intimidating Germany, *Dreadnought* has rather backfired on us. Telegraphs went immediately from Constantinople to Prince Henry, the Kaiser's

younger brother, commander of the High Seas Fleet. He has ordered the Wilhelmshaven Imperial Shipyard to construct half a dozen identical battleships for the Kaiserliche Marine. Henceforth we must converse upon how we should conduct ourselves in a European war, no longer how a war can be avoided. It will bring in the whole of our Empire and shake it like a terrier shakes a rat in a wheat-field. The much-feared East Wind has begun to blow. I doubt if England will spring out from it the wiser and better.'

I turned to the final page.

'Inadvertently, Sherlock, you have put me to work. I am to piece together a plan, a War Book, at the instance of Haldane, the Secretary of State for War. This War Book will be a first in our Island nation's long history. As yet no-one has the slightest idea what happens if a major European war breaks out. Which branch of the Royal Navy will, within minutes of the Declaration, slice through the German undersea cables and cripple their communications to the outside world? Can we blockade Germany in the face of the gathering might of the Kaiserliche Marine? What if the Sauerkraut eaters use their Zeppelins as bombers and scouts? What if they drop poison gas on French and English cities—do we retaliate in kind? I don't believe Lloyd George or Winston Churchill will hesitate a moment. When do we start cutting down iron railings to melt down for our munitions factories? When do we introduce rationing? Should we prepare an evacuation plan for coastal towns? How do we coordinate our railways so that cram-full trains carrying troops south from Scotland and the North to the coasts of Kent and Sussex don't collide with trains hurrying our imports of food west to east, from the docks at Bristol and Liverpool to London? How do we raise a million men in short order—equip them, supply them, transport them to the Continent? How soon should we think the unthinkable—get the fairer sex out of their kitchens into the factories to replace men lost fighting for King and Country? Where do we find tens, perhaps hundreds of thousands of horses? What if the harvest season approaches when the guns begin to fire? It takes three good horses to pull a single harvester. We can hardly remove every horse from every small-holding and still bring in the size of crop we need to feed a country of forty-five million human-beings, surrounded as we shall be by German mines floating on our seas and German boats like grey sharks beneath them, and German airships above. The loss of a horse will become of greater tactical concern than the loss of a human soldier. 'Childer's shocker *The Riddle of the Sands* predicting a German plan to invade our green and pleasant land has frightened the general public beyond all rationality. Who will neutralise the German spies around our Docks and Army bases and seaside towns like Hastings? The parish peeler? The *Daily Mail* reports there are 65,000 German spies in Britain, mostly waiters and hairdressers, each hiding a monocle in his back pocket. We can't fit them all in the Tower. Do keep a close watch on the bushes on your walks on the South Downs.

'I start work on the War Book in the morning—the last first, what shall we put in the precautionary telegram to send around the Empire, that within days, perhaps hours, England will be at war?

'Shall we say lunch soon at the Automobile Club? They are thinly populated at this season.

'I remain, even more, dear Sherlock, your admiring brother.

'Mycroft.

'P.S.—Ironically I have been offered a KCMG for 'services rendered' to foreign affairs. I shan't refuse. We must celebrate. I have a bottle of Imperial Tokay said to be from Franz Joseph's special cellar at the Schoenbrunn Palace.

'P.P.S.—Pity about Shelmerdine. Have you heard? *Mortuus est*. An hour after your departure, at exactly a quarter past nine, a cannon was fired. Shelmerdine was on Galata Bridge. At that instant a deadeye as skilled as a Boer sniper hit him in the head. According to a nearby fisher (who seems now to have fled the city) the shot was fired from the slopes on which Yildiz sits. What remained of Shelmerdine's head would have fitted in a coffee-cup. The fellow was spared *peine forte et dure* at least. *Tarik*, the official organ of the Ottoman government, mourned the passing of a "well-known Stambouli from deadly Syrian malaria". You would be in error if you assume Shelmerdine was a double-agent. He was, strictly speaking, not. He adopted the religion and ways of his targets but acted separately on different issues for different masters.

'His Imperial Majesty has sent condolences to the widow and four children. It means the flow of completely fake expressions of loyalty telegraphed to Abd-ul-Hamid from every quarter of the Ottoman Empire has come to a juddering halt, at least for a while. Shelmerdine was originally commissioned by the Sultan Valide to write them as from ordinary citizens. The practice continued upon her demise with the patronage of the Sultan's Ministers.'

According to Shelmerdine's successor, newly appointed as Mycroft's agent, hardly two hours after I presented the Sultan with the powerful Ross military binoculars the gift had been put to use. A deaf eunuch lip-read my conversation with the dragoman at the landing-pier while the cases and cages were being loaded on the boat. Every word I spoke was relayed to the Palace. The instant I called out, bitingly, 'But don't worry, the skeleton in your closet is perfectly safe with us' I had inadvertently betrayed his true role to the Palace. Shelmerdine was doomed. The death of Mycroft's paid agent—and my central role in it—horrified me. Had I not felt so overwhelming an urge to prove the man had failed to bamboozle the greatest 'gumshoe' in Europe, Shelmerdine would have survived. Even reading my lips would have been more difficult if the custom for medical officers at sea hadn't obliged me to shave my moustache.

* * *

The party by the lake dispersed. My comrade rejoined me. The Foreign Secretary and the Clutterbucks went back to the house to change for Dinner. Holmes pointed at the letter.

'Did you notice Mycroft had the misfortune to get a smear of ink upon the outer side of his right *digitus minimus*?'

I passed the pages back to him to read and waited in silence. He cocked an eye at me.

'You look mournful, Watson.'

'Aren't you dismayed by the news about Shelmerdine?' I asked with some asperity. 'After all, he was an excellent companion. So what if he was involved in a plot to overthrow the Sultan—*if* he was.'

'I might normally be disturbed,' came Holmes's enigmatic reply. 'Except...'

'Except what?' I interrupted.

'Except for the fact he met his fate on Galata Bridge.'

'Galata Bridge?' I echoed. 'How would it matter if he was shot crossing a bridge or climbing the Mountains of the Moon?'

'Not any old bridge. *The* bridge. Also, if you return to the letter, Mycroft doesn't say he was shot crossing the bridge. It only says he was *on* the bridge when he was shot.'

'I know this will shake your confidence in me to the very core, Holmes,' I retorted, 'but I haven't the faintest idea what you're talking about. What difference does it make if he was crossing the bridge or just standing on it?'

My comrade's thin fingers tapped at the letter.

'We are told the shot came from 'the slopes on which Yildiz sits', a distance of several hundred yards.'

'So?'

'Even for a rifle with a state-of-the-art scope and chamber pressure of 20 tons a square inch it's a considerable range.'

Holmes was right. It was a very considerable distance to hit any sort of moving target. My years in India hunting the occasional man-eating tiger had taken place in the jungle, invariably at close range, where jungle-craft and steady nerves were more important than long-range marksmanship.

'For the bullet to strike someone in the head he had to be standing as motionless as a pillar of salt—and for several seconds,' Holmes continued. 'But you saw the fishermen jerking about as though they suffered from Saint Vitus Dance.'

'So?' I pursued.

'Why would our dragoman be standing so still?'

'How do *you* explain it,' I demanded.

'Cast your mind back to the newspaper photograph which revealed our presence to the whole of Stamboul.'

'What has that to do with Shelmerdine?'

Holmes laughed, delighted at my perplexed expression.

'Watson, your bafflement is a perennial delight. In a word—everything! The revelation of our true identity has everything to do with Shelmerdine. How many people knew we were disguised as Royal Naval officers?'

'A good number. I counted Grey and the Prime Minister, your brother Mycroft. Fisher at the Admiralty. The Commodore. Three or four of the most senior officers aboard *Dreadnought*. The Sultan's close entourage. And, yes, Shelmerdine.'

'Excellent, Watson! Fifteen at least. Now tell me, who knew we would choose to go ashore when the entire crew from Commodore downwards was on deck awaiting the arrival of the Royal barge? Which of them knew we would be stepping off the ship *at that moment*? Someone was ready and waiting with a camera. Only one person other than Mycroft and the Commodore knew *in advance* both our assumed naval ranks and that you and I would quit the ship at that exact time. That person was…?'

'Shelmerdine!' I exclaimed, my certainty badly shaken. 'We'd arranged to meet him at 8 o'clock.'

'I'm surprised you didn't note the state of his boots that first time we met him. If he'd taken the carriage straight from his dwelling why would they have been so covered with dust and horse-droppings? I'll wager he was shot taking a photograph of *Dreadnought*'s departure exactly where he took the newspaper photo of us jumping into the *Haroony*. The Sultan's spies would have been well-acquainted with Shelmerdine's custom of setting up his tripod at that very spot.'

I stood in silence while my companion tapped tobacco into his briar.

'Poetic justice, Watson,' Holmes resumed. 'He told us

he'd converted to Mohammedism. If he'd benefit by it he would switch to any belief—Gnosticism, Yarsanism, Samaritanism, Shabakism, Ishikism, Ali-Illahism, Zoroastrianism. Even Buddhism. A man of such expediency can have many masters and will take many sides, sometimes simultaneously. Nevertheless he is due our thanks. By revealing our presence he enabled us to catch Saliha Naciye. The news that Sherlock Holmes had arrived in Stamboul panicked Saliha Naciye into snatching the sword before the engraver could complete his work.'

'The treachery of it all!' I exclaimed indignantly. 'Shelmerdine must have known that revealing our arrival might have laid us open to assassination.'

'As you say,' Holmes returned.

'There's something else which mystifies me, Holmes. Why did Saliha Naciye engineer Mehmed's murder *before* we snared her? I can see why she might...'

'It was essential to cover her tracks. Not even a Sultan's wife could gain access to the sword. She needed Mehmed's help. Until she saw the ghillie suit and hit upon the idea of becoming a spectre she had no way to carry out her plan other than through an alliance with him. He hedged his bets and pretended to be her accomplice. After that, Saliha Naciye needed only one other—the Daughter of Jerusalem. The Jewess's life too might have been in danger except for her enduring value as the principal negotiator with whichever band of conspirators would agree to terms in exchange for the sword. Once Saliha Naciye had hold of the sword Mehmed was not only unnecessary for her plans, he was a definite threat. He could blackmail her—even be a witness against her if the need arose to save himself. It's not impossible it was Chiarezza who pointed this out.'

'Did Mehmed know the Sultan's wife was the spectre?'

'I doubt it. She had no need to tell him. His fear was genuine.'

'What aroused your suspicions about Shelmerdine?'

'The photographs. First, the German submarine. A camera could have been placed almost anywhere along the length of the bridge. However, soon enough I realised it was taken from the exact vantage point as the picture in the newspaper of us getting into the pinnace. Then, if you recall, after we caught Saliha Naciye *in flagrante*, we took another look at the photograph Shelmerdine handed to us on our arrival, the close-up of the sword.'

'What about it?'

'The real sword had already been spirited away.'

He waved Mycroft's letter at me.

'"Shanghaied" as my brother said. Our dragoman must have considered providing us with a snapshot of the unfinished fake but he couldn't risk it. He may have heard we inspected the sword in the oil painting. The snapshot he supplied had to be identical. He could only have taken that photograph if he had access to where they'd sequestered the real thing.'

After a pause he added, 'And then there was the incident at the necropolis.'

'Which incident is that?'

'When Mehmed's widow incriminated our dragoman.'

Marsh as deep as Grimpen Mire on the Devon moors was threatening to engulf me.

'I don't recall her doing anything of the sort,' I replied.

'But you do recall her telling us about the conspiratorial gaggle which met at her house for several nights?'

'Yes.'

'She said they were led by a man anxious to hide his identity behind a hood?'

'I remember that, but…'

'And that the man with us in the cemetery was that same person?'

'I'm certain she said nothing of the…' I spluttered.

'…when she switched to French to cut out any chance her words would be deliberately misreported. She looked at Shelmerdine and said 'Comme lui'.'

'"Comme lui'?' I parroted. 'What of it? Shelmerdine was standing right by her. If she pointed up at him it was because he too wore a hood to hide his face.'

'You wrote down her exact words, Watson. She said, "Those men, those men who were carrying him. I have seen some of them before. They were at my house. Always at night. I saw all their faces, except the man in charge. He wore a hood over his face. 'Comme lui'." But we were all wearing identical hoods. If it were simply the fact the leader of the plotters wore a hood like ours she would have used the plural and said "Comme *vous*", referring to the three of us. She didn't. She was warning us. She recognised him as the man in authority she'd observed in her own home. She deliberately used the singular—comme *lui*—to warn us. Our dragoman realised this immediately. You recall him jumping in with "Perhaps Allah will grant you a son from your last night with your husband—that is, *if you escape with your head intact*". He was letting her know he could have her killed if she didn't fall silent.'

'If you're right, why did Shelmerdine risk accompanying us to the cemetery?'

'The Chief Armourer had been poisoned. The conspirators had no idea who'd been instrumental in Mehmed's death. They had to find out if they were about to be identified.'

'If Shelmerdine did publish the photo in the *Journal de Constantinople*,' I began, 'why on earth…?'

'We were a present danger. His conspiracy was well advanced. By betraying our arrival he hoped we'd decide the game wasn't worth the candle. Either we'd flee or Sir Edward would pull us out.'

Holmes looked at me.

'Watson, your weakness is you make a habit of liking people. You cultivate friendship far too fast. What made me suspect Shelmerdine wasn't all he purported to be? I merely kept in mind he was *exactly* what Mycroft purported him to be.'

He paused, pondering.

'Nevertheless our dragoman was never the *capo dei capi* of the plot. You can tell old Masters by the sweep of their brush. Behind Shelmerdine spun a being on a quite different intellectual plane, my equal, even my superior. We may never discover who lurked behind him but I tell you, Watson, if I didn't know for a definite fact that Professor Moriarty lies in a watery grave...

'Any plot hatched by Saliha Naciye had to be simplicity itself, Lucrezia Borgian in its ruthlessness and crudity. But the other was a plan of exceptional cleverness. Photographing us from the moment of arrival, knowing we lacked any deep knowledge of naval etiquette, reaped its reward. The forgery, costly as it was, would delay discovery of the theft until the time was ripe.'

Holmes added his own postscript.

'We achieved Sir Edward's goal. The Ottoman Empire will hold, at least for the while. We have kept Abd-ul-Hamid on his throne. I doubt if Saliha Naciye will make a second attempt to push him aside. If she tries again and fails she knows she'll be seen floating in a gunny-sack in the Bosphorus.'

Twilight was descending. It was time to change for dinner.

Holmes reflected as we set off, 'Shelmerdine's death may have been a serious blow to the conspirators in the shadows behind him but our dragoman's demise was a relief to Mehmed's widow. Her life was never going to be safe while he lived.'

Absorbed in thought we walked the hundred yards or so to the sturdy mansion, the loveliest of English homes. The duck with a huge spatulate bill and dark green head which had been standing patiently at our feet waddled alongside.

As we walked, Holmes remarked almost wistfully, 'I wish there were always a few sultans about. It'll be a far duller world without such unscrupulous tradesmen. It might be disputed how far any singular gift in an individual is due to his ancestry rather than his own early training but villainy in the blood takes the strangest forms. A study of Abd-ul-Hamid's family portraits—the line from forehead to upper lip, the arch and droop of the nose—is enough to convert a man to the doctrine of reincarnation. If you pricked Abd-ul-Hamid's head the soul of every sultan before him, back to Osman Ghazi, would come hissing out like gas from a container.'

Not for a second in Stamboul had we given thought to any wider consequences of our actions. Now a particular sentence in Mycroft's letter, that Holmes had 'single-handedly made a great war in Europe inevitable, and within ten years', reverberated in my head. How was my comrade to react to an indictment of such magnitude—and from his own brother?

I walked at Holmes's side in apprehensive silence while he blew smoke rings into the air. On the front lawn some yards from the entrance to Chequers I decided to bring the matter up.

'Holmes,' I began, hesitantly, 'there's something Mycroft...'

'You noted that, did you, Watson?'

'...where Mycroft wrote, 'the much-feared East Wind has begun to blow'.'

Holmes smacked his hand on the letter.

'Not that wretched East Wind! Rather I refer you to where my brother says—and I quote—'we came up against each other for the first time, and you came out in front'!'

I turned to stare at him. Crow's feet were forming around the austere grey eyes in a true and impulsive expression of pure happiness. This was the first deeply heartfelt grin I'd ever seen light up Holmes's face.

He waved the letter. Joyfully he repeated, 'Mycroft admits it—I came out in front!'

With an exultant gesture he said, 'Next week we'll dress, dine and enjoy an evening out. What do you say, a bottle of Montrachet *tête-à-tête* and a fine repast—none of your Everyman cut-off-the-joint-and-two-veg served by flat-footed old waiters in greasy dress-coats! We'll start at that most restful temple of food, Simpson's-in-the-Strand, Grand Divan Tavern. *Die Meistersinger von Nürnberg* is on at Covent Garden. If we hurry our meal we might get there just in time for Sachs' full-bellied cobbling song.'

'The *Meistersinger* on you, Holmes?' I asked.

My surgery, wound-pension and fewer and fewer royalties from my publishers all lumped together hardly stretched to getting my silk grosgrain opera hat and dress boots cleaned and the cost of a ticket for a Wagnerian comedy, let alone a splendid repast at Simpson's.

'Better still, my dear friend...' He tapped a bulge in his pocket. '...on His Majesty King Edward's Government! Our Foreign Secretary was as good as his word. We have a considerable number of five jacks to share. Once more you'll dine on smoked Scottish salmon, followed by treacle sponge with Madagascan vanilla custard — the very dishes I believe you ordered at the start of the case of the Bulgarian Codex.'

The memory of Stamboul was fading, its kaleidoscope

of colour and sights, the stench of rubbish piled up in the streets, the smell of rotting fish pervading the quayside, the manifold grotesqueries and intrigues. Even my primal terror in the face of the gastromancy.

'And your dish?' I asked.

'I too shall order as I ordered then,' he replied, 'slices of roast beef delivered on a silver trolley. Perhaps, as then, another anonymous note will be delivered in a Bon Bon dish,' adding with an uncommon self-mockery, 'written with a J pen on royal cream paper.'

The bit was clearly between his teeth.

'If so, I shall quit my bees and you your chambers. We shall set off once more, like the scourging hounds of hell.'

* * *

The weeks went by. The intense colours of high summer in Stamboul were overtaken by the cooler palette of memory running from silver and horse-back browns to perse. The Michaelmas daisies in Regent's Park with their mass of misty purples came and went. Holmes had long since returned to the quietude of his bee-farm. My moustache had re-established itself.

Heavily bundled-up, I took a morning constitutional around the boating-lake in Regent's Park. A question kept repeating in my mind. Moments before Holmes set off from the Ottoman shore that last time he astounded me by identifying Shelmerdine as the principal abettor in the second plot. He swore me to secrecy. His exact words were, 'Watson, it must remain our secret, yours and mine, do you understand?' As he flung himself aboard the tender and set off for *Dread-*

nought he even added, 'Shelmerdine remains of paramount value to England'. Within minutes I had broken my word. Within hours Shelmerdine was dead. Holmes's reticence was a familiar and often frustrating characteristic. Why, I now asked myself, hadn't he kept the startling revelation to himself until I rejoined him aboard the battleship?

Standing there in the damp air of Regent's Park the rose-tinted glasses through which I had long viewed my old friend were quickly becoming less rosy. He knew I would wait behind at the dockside until Shelmerdine brought Mycroft's spices and returned my camera. The fact Holmes did not bide his time could mean only one thing: he had determined, correctly, that my affectionate regard for all things Holmesian would tempt me into a serious indiscretion. He *meant* me to reveal all to the dragoman. To use one of my comrade's own phrases it was the only conclusion I could come to, 'consistent with sanity'.

I felt as stunned as if I'd been struck from behind by a Penang lawyer wielded by a dacoit. It would have occurred to Holmes that the Palace would have us in its eye to the very moment we quit the Empire's shores. It was *Holmes*, purposefully, not I inadvertently, who set in motion the shot that dropped the dragoman on Galata Bridge.

As I walked past the Heronry a second dramatic thought struck me. What role had Holmes's brother Mycroft really played? The public disclosure of our identity through the flaming headlines in the Stambouli newspaper could not have been left to a dragoman's initiative. Shelmerdine may have published the photograph of our arrival but only on specific orders. Whose orders? Was Mycroft the advance-agent of a movement so epoch-making that not one Englishman in fifty thousand would ever dream of it—to dismantle the Ottoman Empire with all speed and at any cost?

A casual rumour picked up—even invented—by the Diogenes Club concerning the Sword of Osman could have been transmitted back to the bazaars via provocateurs like Shelmerdine, to be acted upon by Saliha Naciye and the CUP or the rival Prince Sabahedrinne. Mycroft was aware the sword had been shanghaied before our arrival. He must have been in constant telegraphic communication with our dragoman. The meeting between Sir Edward Grey and Sherlock Holmes at the Foreign Secretary's initiative must have come as a bombshell for Holmes's brother. Mycroft's letter delivered by special messenger to our train at Victoria with its mumbo jumbo about a new Convention on spies positively begged us to wiggle our way out of the case before it commenced. Looking back it seemed astonishing we weren't assassinated the moment the *Journal de Constantinople* revealed our presence. The last undercover person fitted out by Gieves as an Army doctor intent, supposedly, on studying the use of vegetables in Ottoman medicine never made it back. We would have offered the simplest of targets for Shelmerdine's co-conspirators at the crowded waterside. The open graves at the cemetery could have been dug specially for us. Our throats could have been slit in an instant when we confronted the Chief Armourer's widow in the grove.

Had we once more lived a charmed life? Or were we allowed to live because Holmes was Mycroft's younger sibling?

Postscript

Several readers kindly asked after Philip Jacobus Pretorius. They recalled how the summons from Holmes to meet Edward Grey led to the abandonment of my planned visit to the great jungles of central Africa. Subsequent obligations led to further postponements until, as happens, the entire enterprise fell away, to be dreamed about on cold winters' evenings. Soon after the outbreak of the Great War a letter arrived from Pretorius, by then an officer in the British Imperial Government attached to Admiral King-Hall. To enlist in the service Pretorius had had to escape from German-occupied territory in East Africa, undergoing an ordeal in the vast jungles quite unparalleled in my own experience, despite my warring years in the deadly Frontier Tribal Areas of British India. His exceptional scouting skills were to lead to the hunt for the German raider *SMS Königsberg*, a light cruiser of the Kaiser's Imperial Navy named after the Capital of Prussia. On 20 September 1914 she surprised and sank the British protected cruiser *HMS Pegasus* in the Battle of Zanzibar. With Pretorius's involvement, revenge was soon to hand.

The End

Notes From The Author

My Endpieces seem to grow in length with each succeeding Sherlock Holmes adventure I write. Kindly readers tell me they enjoy reading this section but of course you do not need to bother. I add them simply for interest and colour. I list the books I have read as background including memoirs of the Edwardian age in England and Turkey. Some of the writing is so atmospheric I incorporate small bits into Holmes's and Watson's Stamboul adventure. I have also tended to use the spelling current in the Edwardian period, so for example Mombasa was often Mombassa, diplomats spelt Baghdad without the 'h', hence Bagdad, and Kiev as Kieff, and the 's' many British now prefer to use in words like 'civilisation' was then a 'z', like the USA today.

Readers of my other 'sherlocks' will have realised I have very considerable admiration for Dr. John H. Watson. There's no doubt the Sultan was correct. If Watson had not taken on the task of chronicling Holmes's cases, the latter's career as a Great Detective may never have taken off. It was sheer kismet the former Army doctor on a wound-pension needed to find and share the cost of digs in London in 1881 at the precise time the peripatetic young Sherlock Holmes did too. I have little time for the Basil Rathbone/Nigel Bruce depiction as a well-intentioned bumbler, loyal but clueless. Watson said of himself, 'If I have one quality upon earth it is common sense'.

He was also eager, chivalrous and courageous. Much more than Holmes he was like his creator Arthur Conan Doyle. Like Doyle, Watson had the qualities of a good doctor—kindliness, optimism and a healthy scepticism. Watson had another value to Holmes. Medicine is said to be as much the ability to gain the confidence of the patient as it is an abstract science.

'Your best friends would hardly call you a schemer, Watson,' Holmes told him, adding later, 'I never get to your limits. There are unexplored possibilities about you.'

It's not possible to trace the various paths by which Conan Doyle himself created Watson. While writing these notes I was on the train to London Charing Cross from deepest East Sussex reading *The Crooked Scythe* by George Ewart Evans, an anthology of memories of men and women of a past era—farm labourers, shepherds, horsemen, blacksmiths, wheelwrights, sailors, fisherman, miners, maltsters, domestic servants. The introduction by a David Gentleman described the author Evans as follows:

'George was in his mid-fifties when I first saw him… upright and vigorous, with an open and friendly manner and a clear, piercing gaze. He looked the part of a countryman, in a tweed jacket, a hat also of tweed, drill trousers, and stout brown shoes. As I grew to know him, I discovered that he was sympathetic and generous with help and encouragement. He was intelligent and shrewd; his judgements, though seldom sharply expressed, were acute and rational. In conversation he was tolerant and unassertive, but it was soon clear he held independent views with firmness and conviction.'

I'm certain this is how Watson's many friends at the Junior United Services club and at the Gatwick races would have viewed him too, a man of gentility though of limited means and no property. We should all have friends who wear stout brown shoes.

At several points in this new adventure I mention Watson's unfulfilled plans to go to Africa ('the Dark Continent with its great herds of elephants, odd-toed ungulates on the Luangwa, hippo on the Shire River, the Tsavo man-eating lions, dust, blood, sleeping sickness, malaria, alcoholism, the smell of camp-fires long extinguished...'). Writing about his plans took me back nostalgically to my own late-teenage years in East and Central Africa. One day I shall get Watson there too.

Miscellany

Abd-ul-Hamid 11 (22 September 1842—10 February 1918). Variously spelt Abdul Hamid and Abdülhamid. 34th Sultan of the Ottoman Empire. An article in the Manchester Guardian on July 24 1905 reported an attempt on the Sultan's life when he attended the Mosque. Titled 'The Sultan's Escape', the Manchester Guardian commented, 'Judging by the number killed (the majority of them soldiers lining the road near the Mosque) and by the material damage, the bomb used must have been a formidable engine... the Sultan preserved the most remarkable sang froid, although a wild panic ensued among the onlookers...'

In an Editorial Article the same day, the Manchester

Guardian opined, 'There is hardly a race in Turkey but has its grounds for vengeance, and few living creatures in all the Empire who would not rejoice in the Sultan's death, unless, perhaps, the dogs in the Stamboul streets that owe their lives to his capricious and incalculable mercies...The whole Osmanli brood is tainted by its prison-palace life, degenerate, uneducated, and incapable of resisting the influence of the counter-spies who manage it.'

In the summer of 1908, the Young Turk Revolution broke out. On being told troops in Salonika were advancing on him, Abd-ul-Hamid capitulated. The last Sultan to exert autocratic control over the Ottoman Empire, he was deposed by the parliament on April 26 1909 and conveyed into captivity at Salonika ('that city of vipery', he had called it). In 1912, when Salonika fell to Greece, he was returned to captivity in Constantinople. Just as he (and Shelmerdine) had predicted, in World War One the Young Turks threw their lot in with Kaiser Wilhelm's Germany. The 34th Sultan spent his last days studying, carpentering and writing his memoirs in custody at Beylerbeyi Palace in the Bosphorus, where he died on 10 February 1918, the year the Ottoman Empire collapsed. He was buried in a mausoleum along with Sultans Mahmud II and Abdülaziz near Sultanahmet Square. His obituary appeared in *The Times*.

Rahime Perestu Sultan (1830–1904) was the Circassian wife of Ottoman Sultan Abdülmecid I and Valide Sultan during the reign of Abd-ul-Hamid II. She was the last Valide Sultan of the Ottoman Empire. Her burial place is located at the tomb of Mihrişah Valide Sultan in Eyüp, a part of

Istanbul. The name Perestu means peacock in Persian. She became the spiritual mother of Sultan Abd-ul-Hamid 11.

Valide Sultan, literally 'mother sultan', was the title held by the queen mother of a ruling Sultan of the Ottoman Empire, first used in the 16th century for Ayşe Hafsa Sultan, consort of Selim I and mother of Suleiman the Magnificent. As the mother to the sultan the Valide Sultan had a significant influence on the affairs of the empire.

Saliha Naciye (born circa 1882), a Georgian, thirteenth and last wife of Sultan Abd-ul-Hamid 11. He married her on 4 November 1904 at Yıldız Palace. Saliha Naciye accompanied Abd-ul-Hamid into exile and returned to Istanbul with him in 1912. She died on 4 December 1923 in a mansion located at Erenköy and was buried near the mausoleum of Sultan Mahmud II, located at Divan Yolu Street. She was about the age of forty-one.

Crown Prince Mehmed Abid Efendi, Abd-ul-Hamid's son by Saliha Naciye, died in Beirut in 1973 and was buried in Damascus.

Sir Edward Grey. He continued to serve as Foreign Secretary until 1916, up to then the longest continuous tenure of any person in that office. Best remembered for his remark at the outbreak of the First World War: 'The lamps are going out all over Europe. We shall not see them lit again in our life-time'. History knows the lamps flickered back on for a brief period after 1918, to be extinguished in 1939 by the murderous Adolph Hitler.

Sir Edward was ennobled as Viscount Grey of Fallodon in 1916. In 1919 he became Ambassador to the United

States, and later Leader of the Liberal Party in the House of Lords. His interest in nature began early, on his father's estate at Falloden. Probably inspired by his first wife Dorothy's knowledge of bird-song, he joined the Royal Society for the Protection of Birds in 1893 and became a Vice-President in 1909.

In 1927, Hodder and Stoughton published Grey's *The Charm of Birds*. It was an immediate popular success and still widely read and admired. Grey's second wife Pamela's contribution to *The Charm of Birds* can be seen in her description of the dawn chorus and of a goldfinch nesting among apple blossom.

In 1928 Grey was made Chancellor of Oxford University although his own academic background had been slight—'rusticated' from Baliol though he returned to take a lowly Third in Jurisprudence.

He died in 1933.

Sir Peter Chalmers Mitchell CBE FRS DSc LLD (23 November 1864–2 July 1945), zoologist, was Secretary of the Zoological Society of London from 1903 to 1935. He directed the policy of the London Zoo, and created Whipsnade, the world's first open zoological park. He died in July 1945 after being knocked down outside the north gate of London Zoo.

Henry Morton Stanley (28 January 1841-May 1904). Born John Rowlands, he was a Welsh journalist and explorer famous for his exploration of central Africa and his search for missionary and explorer David Livingstone. Upon finding Livingstone, Stanley later claimed he uttered the now-famous greeting, 'Dr. Livingstone, I presume?'. Stanley is also known for his discoveries and development of the Congo region.

Major Percy Horace Gordan Powell-Cotton (1866-1940). Elephant hunter. The largest African elephant he shot carried tusks weighing 372lbs, one tusk being over 9 feet in length and more than two feet in circumference. The world may never see the like of such an elephant again, the more's the pity, though most likely poachers would seek it out and kill it.

Acknowledgments

My great thanks to –

Lesley Abdela, my partner, for her ever-warm encouragement and interest in these adventures. As I wrote in my first novel in 2012, she has taken on work assignments at great risk to her life in distant, war-torn places like Iraq and Afghanistan, and now turbulent places like Egypt and Ukraine, to bring in an income while I tap away on a laptop in the beautiful woods around Burwash, in the Sussex High Weald, not too far from where Holmes bought his bee-farm, or in successive Septembers on the island of Gavdos in the Aegean for the final run-through of the text.

Steve Emecz, Managing Director, MX Publishing. A hero to over 100 Sherlock Holmes authors, including me. MX is the largest publisher of Sherlock Holmes stories in the world, many of them now being translated into other languages including Russian. MX is a tremendous asset to the United Kingdom and to everyone who likes to escape from the everyday real world for a while, accompanying Holmes and Watson on their great adventures.

Ailsa Crofts in far-away Scotland for her sterling work editing 'The Sword', cutting down on excesses and diversions which creep into the text as I build it into a full-length novel. And to Rosie Grupp whose professional skill has made the layout so aesthetically pleasing and easy on the eye.

Dr. Judith Rowbotham. Yet again this exceptional historian of Victorian crime has performed her wonders for *The Sword of Osman* whenever I have needed information and background. Her expertise ranges far beyond crime alone. She put together the Foreign Secretary's outfit in one of the important scenes where he attempts to hide his identity at the Regent's Park Zoological Gardens, and provided insights into the risks taken by Holmes and Watson masquerading as naval officers while on a diplomatic mission for the British Government at the time the 1907 Hague Convention on the laws of war was being finalised.

Heather Johnson, The National Museum Library, Royal Navy, Portsmouth. Heather's and her colleagues' unstinting assistance in technical matters concerning the Royal Navy in 1906 added immensely to the sheer fun in writing a novel set in the past. For example: 'There is about 15 fathoms depth of water in the Golden Horn, which is essentially non-tidal and is sufficient for depth purposes. The B Class submarines were new in 1906 and capable of being deployed to the Mediterranean, indeed some were in action later in Turkish waters including the Dardanelles but the battery life and submersion time was limited. As for a mock battle, this would only really be viable with any accompanying ships in the squadron. If *Dreadnought* is accompanied by escorts then something might be arranged, this could be made most impressive by rapid firing of the 12lb anti-torpedo craft guns and a limited number of shots from the big guns. Equally viable would be a practice shoot against some form of agreed upon target, bearing in mind that the blast of the main turret guns could cause damage and/or discomfort to observers such that the Sultan and entourage would need to be on the bridge.'

Eric Shelmerdine M.A.B.I.W.A.D. General Secretary of the Association of British Investigators. With his permission I have used his name and turned him into the dragoman who tried his best to bamboozle Holmes. Eric, whenever you're in Turkey don't stand for too long on the Galata Bridge.

Professor Benjamin Fortna, Historian of the Modern Middle East at SOAS, University of London. A world expert on the final years of the Ottoman Empire. His special research focus on the late Ottoman Empire and the early Turkish Republic was both gripping and valuable as background to my plot.

Robert Ribeiro. Again my thanks for his eagle (and lawyerly) eye in reading through the typescript and offering valuable suggestions on terminology and matters of historical fact. And to his wife Professor Aileen Ribeiro, author of many books and articles on the history of dress, the most recent being *Fashion and Fiction. Dress in Art and Literature in Stuart England* (Yale: 2005). Their house in Sussex was built and lived in by the illustrator Walter Paget, brother of Sidney Paget whose portrayals in *The Strand* formed the world's physical impression of the Great Detective—complete with deerstalker.

Jeff Sobel for his extraordinary knowledge of armaments, not least the weaponry Watson has recourse to. Jeff's father, Dean Eli Sobel, was the ever-helpful Head of Department when I was an undergrad and grad student at UCLA.

Sara Wise for her superb review in *The Lancet* of the Museum of London's Sherlock Holmes Exhibition 2014/2015 *Sherlock Holmes: The Man Who Never Lived and*

Will Never Die, at www.thelancet.com/journals/lancet/article/PIIS0140-6736%2814%2962325-4/fulltext#

Elisabeth Thurlow, Archivist, Guardian News & Media, for the historical information from the Manchester Guardian on the attempt on the Sultan's life in July 1905.

Cdr Peter White RN Ret., Britannia Association. This master of the Royal Navy's complex etiquette gave me the idea for the important scene where Holmes and Watson are revealed as counterfeit naval officers. As Commander White explained, on short journeys a naval sword is always carried and never hooked up. To get on or off a pinnace, the 'Senior Officer's Carry' would be employed. Holmes and Watson didn't know this arcane bit of naval etiquette… with unexpected results.

Paul Smith, Thomas Cook's Archivist, for mapping out Holmes's and Watson's journey from London to Gibraltar in 1906, according to the May 1906 edition of Cook's Continental Timetable. A final journey by steamer would have brought the pair to Gibraltar. The minimum time required for this journey was 104 hours.

Michael Pritchard FRPS, Director General of the Royal Photographic Society, coming up trumps on photography of the period. It was he who brought to my attention the Sultan's Adams quarter-plate De Luxe hand camera with red-leather covered body and 18 carat gold fittings, the most expensively produced camera in the world.

Michael Palmer, Archivist & Deputy Librarian, Zoological Society of London for great help concerning the lay-out of the Regent's Park Zoo in 1906. The Birdhouse at London

Zoo: although the building that is now the Bird House did exist in 1906, it was built and used as the Reptile House until 1927, when it was converted to the use of birds.

Dr Robert Elgood. SOAS Department of the History of Art and Archaeology. World expert and Research Fellow on Eastern European, Islamic and Asian Arms and Armour. Was at the Wallace Collection 2006-2012.

Menelaos Danellis. Researcher and collector of Ottoman period bladed weapons and firearms volunteering at the Middle East Department of the British Museum. His advice on *The Sword of Osman* enabled Holmes to recognise the forgery and identify the ringleader of the plot.

Robert Pooley of Pooley Sword Ltd. 'Yes, we make special presentation Swords, particularly for Arabia. If anyone has the money (considerable), we could certainly reproduce almost exactly the Sword of Osman. What you have to bear in mind with a forgery is not only has the Swordsmith got to copy the blade exactly but so has the engraver. When it comes to the crosspiece and the grip and pommel, this is very much the work of a Silversmith or Goldsmith of some distinction. To copy something is probably harder than making an original.'

Katherine Owen, Woodland Trust Ancient Woodland Restoration Engagement Manager, and Owen Johnson who compiled the Collins tree guide for Europe, for advice on trees in Turkey.

Mrs Jane VS Wickenden, MA (Oxon), DipLib. Historic Collections Librarian, Institute of Naval Medicine, for example for the description of Dr. Watson's uniform aboard HMS Dreadnought: 'The most distinctive part of a Surgeon

RN's uniform would be (as it still is) the red distinction cloth between the gold stripes—there would have been no "curl" at that date, and no rank division such as Surgeon Commander.'

Sophie Wilcox, librarian at the Alexander Library of Ornithology, Edward Grey Institute. http://libguides.bodleian. ox.ac.uk/alexanderlibrary who recommended such valuable reference books as *Bird Wonders of the Zoo*, by Lilian Gask. 1911, and *The Avifauna of British India and its Dependencies*, by James A. Murray. 1888/1890.

Lorna Cahill, Library, Art and Archives, Stuart Cable, Herbarium, and Christopher Mills, all at the Royal Botanic Gardens, Kew, for wonderful help in tracing plants which may have found their way to the Sultan's herbarium and gardens at Yildiz.

Professor Alan Dronsfield, Royal Society of Chemistry Historical Group, for his valuable knowledge of the luminous paint of yesteryear incorporated in the ghost scene.

Dr Anne B Hodgson, Department of Chemistry, University of York, suggesting the ghost's outfit (the ghillie suit) should be rubberised for the safety of the human inside it. (Scottish gamekeepers, don't try Saliha Naciye's ruse at home)

Dave Johnson, Wildlife Officer/Bird Keeper, Royal Parks for his help on bird-life in Regent's Park in the Edwardian period.

Elizabeth Loder and Kristina Fister of the British Medical Journal for valuable help in researching the Victorian approach to 'puerperal mania'.

Prof Liz Bentley of the Royal Meteorological Society for

providing weather details for May 1906 when Dr. Watson went to Regent's Park. 'There were some rather warm days early that May, and the temperature on the 8th almost reached 23°C. However, thundery rain followed overnight with nearly 20mm recorded. It then became much cooler, and on the 10th, the maximum temperature was only 9.8°C.'

Wesley Horton of Claremore, Oklahoma, who supplied really interesting information on his collection of code books, many acquired from the Central Code Bureau.

Howard White of Hastings who continues to drop by to chew over my latest plot and scouts out the settings I've used around the Sussex Weald and South Downs.

Last (but far from least), my unending thanks to Wikipedia, Google and the Encyclopaedia Britannica for putting most of the world at the touch of a keyboard, even in the very depths of the woodland in England's High Weald where I retreat on sunny days with my laptop and canvas folding-chair. By contrast when a novelist uncle of mine, Elleston Trevor (*Flight of the Phoenix* and the *Quiller* series etc.), started writing in the 1950s, it took him up to a month just to order a book from the library in St. Peter Port for his research—assuming he knew which book he wanted.

Publications

In addition to *The Charm of Birds*, Edward Grey several published books far removed from his official works, such as *Cottage Book* and *The Undiscovered Country Diary of an Edwardian Statesman* (Sir Edward and Lady Dorothy Grey), dedicated to the birds, flowers and trees which enhanced and gave joy to the spring and summers spent in Hampshire.

She, by H. Rider Haggard. First Published 1886. Haggard would have been well-known to every adventurous young man of the Victorian period. He was a founder of the Lost World literary genre. Adventure novels such as *King Solomon's Mines* were set in exotic locations, predominantly Africa. *She,* with 83 million copies sold by 1965, is one of the best-selling books of all time.

Well worth reading is a biography of Rider Haggard titled *The Cloak That I Left*, by his daughter Lilias. Boydell Press.

The Unveiled Ladies of Stamboul, by Demetra Vaka. Gorgias Press 2005. First published in 1923. The author was born on the island of Prinkipo, off the coast of Constantinople, and emigrated to America at the age of 17. She returned often to Turkey as a foreign correspondent.

The Rise And Decay Of The Rule Of Islam by Archibald J. Dunn. British Library Historical Print Editions. Like Holmes's brother Mycroft, Sir Edward Grey must have read Dunn's polemic on the Eastern Question expressed in the 1877 edition because he quotes him nearly verbatim when explaining the matter to Holmes and Watson.

The Sherlock Holmes Miscellany, by Roger Johnson & Jean Upton. Foreword by Gyles Brandreth. The History Press. 2012. A beautifully produced book of pocket size, a must for all Sherlockians. www.thehistorypress.co.uk/index.php/the-sherlock-holmes-miscellany.html

Arthur Conan Doyle, A Life In Letters. Harper Perennial 2008. Ed. Jon Lellenberg, Daniel Stashower, Charles Folley. 710pp. Valuable background expressed through Doyle's profuse correspondence, much to his mother Mary.

My Dear Holmes, A Study In Sherlock. Gavin Brend. Allen & Dunwin 1951.

His Last Bow: Some Reminiscences of Sherlock Holmes was published in 1917, a collection of seven previously-published Sherlock Holmes. Five of the stories were published *in The Strand Magazine* between September 1908 and December 1913. The final story, an epilogue about Holmes's war service, was first published in Collier's on 22 September 1917—one month before the book's premier on 22 October. Some later editions of the collection include *The Adventure of the Cardboard Box,* which was also collected in *The Memoirs of Sherlock Holmes* (1894). *The Strand* published *The Adventure of Wistaria Lodge* as *A Reminiscence of Sherlock Holmes,* and divided it into two parts, called *The Singular Experience of Mr. John Scott Eccles* and *The Tiger of San Pedro.* Later printings of *His Last Bow* corrected Wistaria to Wisteria. The first US edition adjusted the subtitle to *Some Later Reminiscences of Sherlock Holmes.*

The Adventure of the Naval Treaty. One of the 56 Sherlock Holmes short stories. Conan Doyle ranked it 19th in a list of his 19 favourite Sherlock Holmes stories. Watson receives a letter from an old schoolmate, now a Foreign Office employee, who has had an important naval treaty stolen from his office. Has the theft been made on behalf of Czarist Russia or France (both perceived at the time to be potential enemies)? *The Naval Treaty* is one of the first in the emerging genre of spy story.

Fly Fishing. On trout, sea trout and salmon. Written by Edward Grey when he was thirty years of age, before his eyesight began to deteriorate sharply. Considered the equal of Walton's much-better-known *Compleat Angler*.

The Charm of Birds. First published in 1927 with woodcuts, it was an immediate popular success. Full of sensitive observation and beautifully written.

Twenty-Five Years 1892-1916, by Viscount Grey of Falloden. Hodder And Stoughton. 1925. Wonderfully written memoires by one of the most famous British Foreign Secretaries. I have used some of his descriptions in *The Sword of Osman*. A must for anyone interested in the period leading to the First World War.

The Sultan, by Joan Haslip. Reissued by Weidenfeld & Nicolson. 1973. Excellent list of illustrations, written in lively style.

The Harem, by N.M.Penzer. Subtitled 'an account of the institution as it existed in the Palace of the Turkish Sultans with a history of the Grand Seraglio from its foundation to modern times'. First published by George G. Harrap & Co. 1936.

Everyday Life in Ottoman Turkey, by Raphaela Lewis. B.T. Batsford Ltd. 1971. Really excellent 206 pages. The part titled 'Portrait of a City' is especially worth reading.

The Best Letters of Lady Mary Wortley Montagu. Edited by Octave Thanet. A. C. McClurg & Co. Second Edition 1901. Lady Mary Wortley Montagu (1689-1762) was the wife of the British Ambassador to Turkey. In 1715 she had survived but been terribly scarred by smallpox while her brother had died from the disease. She was fascinated by the culture of the Ottoman Empire and in 1717 described the Turkish practice of inoculating healthy children with a weakened strain of smallpox to confer immunity from the more virulent strains of the disease. She immediately had her seven-year old son inoculated in Turkey and on her return to England, she had her daughter publicly inoculated at the royal court of George I to popularize the technique. In this she was only partially successful as inoculation continued to be dangerous and often resulted in death and scarring of infected children.

M. Şükrü Hanioğlu. *The Second Constitutional Period, 1908–1918* Volume 4: Turkey in the Modern World. Cambridge Histories Online. Nov. 2009.

Diary of an Idle Woman in Constantinople (1892). For a prevailing, sometimes contemptuous view of Stamboul ('ill-smelling mob') by an itinerant English 'Idle Woman' travel-writer Frances Elliott, see https://archive.org/details/diaryanidlewoma03elligoog

The Sultan and His Subjects Volume 1-2 by Richard Davey. General Books, Memphis, USA.

Lords of the Horizons, A History of the Ottoman Empire, by Jason Goodwin. Chatto & Windus 1998. A lively account of the machinations of the major players in the Ottoman Empire from its origins to its collapse centuries later.

My Mission To Russia And Other Diplomatic Memories, by Sir George Buchanan. Little, Brown And Company. 1923.

With a Field Ambulance At Ypres: Being Letters Written

March 7—August 15, 1915. William Boyd. George H. Doran Company.

In Unknown Africa, by Percy Powell-Cotton, Hurst & Blackett, 1904. An account of a 'wanderer' and collector shooting his way through British East Africa in the Edwardian period.

The Urban Sea, Cities of the Mediterranean, by Dennis Hardy. Blue Gecko Books. 2013. Valuable and nicely-written account ranging across geography and history, with an appeal to a wide audience who visit the various cities around the coast of the world's most famous Sea.

The Life And Times Of Sherlock Holmes, by Philip Weller with Christopher Roden. Studio Editions. 1992. Coffee-table size, packed with illustrations and informative background material.

Conan Doyle, The Man Who Created Sherlock Holmes, by Andrew Lycett. Phoenix. 554pp. 2007. Just about the best book on Doyle himself. Filled with interesting accounts right through Doyle's life, including that 10 horsepower blue Wolseley with red wheels.

The Sherlock Holmes Companion, by Michael and Molly Hardwick. First published 1962 by John Murray, London.

The London of Sherlock Holmes, by Michael Harrison. David & Charles, Newton Abbot. 1972.

A Study In Surmise, by Michael Harrison. Subtitled 'The Making of Sherlock Holmes'. Introduction by Ellery Queen. Gaslight Publications. 1984.

The Sherlock Holmes Scrapbook. New English Library, 1973. Introduction by Peter Cushing.

Investigating Sherlock Holmes by Hartley Nathan and Clifford Goldfarb. Mosaic Press, 2014.

The Influence of Royal Tours on the Conduct of British Diplomacy 1901-1918. Matthew Glencross. PhD Thesis. Argues the importance of royal diplomacy (e.g. Edward V11).

The Foreign Policy of Sir Edward Grey 1906-1915. Gilbert Murray. Forgotten Books. Originally published 1915.

Sherbet & Spice, The Complete Story of Turkish Sweets and Desserts, by Mary Işin. I.B. Tauris. 2013. Turkish cuisine is placed in the highest category of cuisines, alongside French, Italian, Indian and Chinese.

A British Borderland, Service And Sport in Equatoria, by Captain H. A. Wilson. John Murray, 1913. A vivid account of life in deepest East Africa between 1902 and 1906, mostly on the Anglo-German Boundary Commission sorting out where British and German East Africa lay.

Allan Quartermain. The wildly-popular protagonist of H. Rider Haggard's 1885 novel *King Solomon's Mines* and its sequels.

Heart of Darkness (1899). A short novel by Polish novelist Joseph Conrad about the character Charles Marlow's life as an ivory transporter down the Congo River in Central Africa. It was a best-seller almost from the start, and Watson would certainly have read it, along with William Clark Russell's sea stories, the latter author described by Swinburne as 'the greatest master of the sea, living or dead'.

The Adventure of The Bruce-Partington Plans. Set in 1895. The monotony of smog-shrouded London is broken by a sudden visit from Holmes's brother Mycroft. He has come about some missing, secret submarine plans. 'You may take it from me,' said Mr. Holmes's brother in speaking of them, 'that naval warfare becomes impossible when in the radius of a Bruce Partington operation.'

The Riddle of the Sands: A Record of Secret Service' by Erskine Childers. Published in 1903. The book enjoyed immense popularity in the years before World War I and is an early example of the espionage novel, extremely influential in the genre of spy fiction. Childers's biographer Andrew Boyle noted: 'For the next ten years Childers's book remained the most powerful contribution of any English writer to the debate on Britain's alleged military unpreparedness'. It was a notable influence on John Buchan and, much later, Ken Follett.

The Rifle Rangers by Captain Mayne Reid. 'Captain' Mayne Reid's first boys' story, extremely popular in Victorian times. At one point the hero is to die by hanging by the heels over a precipice in south Mexico. At another he and his companions are attacked by a pack of snarling bloodhounds.

The Final Problem. Includes the weird description of Moriarty: '...his face protrudes forward and is forever slowly oscillating from side to side in a curiously reptilian fashion.'—early stages of Shaky Palsy?

The Adventure of Wisteria Lodge. A lengthy, two-part story consisting of *The Singular Experience of Mr. John Scott Eccles* and *The Tiger of San Pedro*, which on original publication in The Strand bore the collective title of *A Reminiscence of Mr. Sherlock Holmes*. Set around 1894 and published in 1908. Of the entire collection of Holmes stories by Doyle, this is the only story in which a police inspector (specifically Inspector Baynes) is acknowledged as competent as Holmes. Contains insights into Holmes's methods, for example, 'There are no better instruments than discharged servants with a grievance, and I was lucky enough to find one. I call it luck, but it would not have come my way had I not been looking out for it.'

Lexicon

Achates. The Sultan was displaying his considerable depth of reading in the Classics. In the Aeneid, Achates ("good, faithful Achates", or fidus Achates as he was called) was a close friend of Aeneas; his name became a by-word for an intimate companion. He accompanied Aeneas throughout his adventures, reaching Carthage with him in disguise when the pair scouted the area.

Aconite. A powerful plant, used in the past as a medicinal herb, a poison and in potions for incantations. Until the 20th century it was the deadliest toxin known. The leaves and root yield its active ingredient, an alkaloid called Aconitine, frequently used to tip hunting darts or javelins. The poison takes effect quickly. In late-Victorian times the poison was made famous by its use in Oscar Wilde's 1891 story Lord Arthur Savile's Crime.

Abus gun is an early form of artillery created by the Ottoman Empire. They were small but heavy to carry. Many were equipped with a type of tripod.

Aristolochia. A genus of evergreen and deciduous woody vines and herbaceous perennials known to contain the lethal toxin aristolochic acid. The plants are aromatic. Their strong scent attracts insects.

Borsalini. Hat company known particularly for its fedoras. Founded by Giuseppe Borsalini in 1857, the felt hats were produced from Belgian rabbit fur at a factory in Alessandria, Italy. When Giuseppe Borsalini died in 1900 his son Teresio succeeded him.

British Empire. Like most Britons of his class and background, Watson was unquestioningly proud of an Empire which comprised the dominions, colonies, protectorates, mandates and other territories ruled or administered by Whitehall. The Empire originated with the overseas possessions and trading posts established by England between the late 16th and early 18th centuries. At its height it was the largest empire in history and for over a century the foremost global power. By 1922, but by then overstretched, the British Empire held sway over about 458 million people, one-fifth of the world's population at the time, covering more than 33,700,000 km2 (13,012,000 sq mi). This was almost a quarter of the Earth's total land area.

Camarilla. A group of courtiers or favourites who surround a ruler. A word used more in Edwardian times than now. Usually, they do not hold any office or have any official authority at court but influence their ruler behind the scenes. Consequently, they also escape having to bear responsibility for the effects of their advice. The term derives from the Spanish word, camarilla (diminutive of cámara), meaning 'little chamber' or private cabinet of the king.

'Chapeau!' The French for hat. I.e. 'Hats off to you!'

Crape (anglicized versions of the French crêpe). Silk, wool, or later polyester fabric of a gauzy texture, with a particular crimpy appearance. Silk crape is woven of hard spun silk yarn in the gum or natural condition. There are two distinct varieties of the textile: soft, Canton, or Oriental crape, and hard or crisped crape.

Dog-dung. The pavements of Constantinople were covered with dung from the hundreds, perhaps thousands of street dogs permitted to live by a quirk of the Sultan's affections. This was very useful to the tanning trade which used dog-dung extensively, hence the many apprentice tanners walking around collecting it.

Dreadnought. HMS Dreadnought revolutionised naval power from the moment of her launch in Portsmouth on 10 February 1906 by King Edward VII at a construction cost in Sterling of £1,783,883 (over GBP£200 million in 2015 terms). She was christened with an Australian wine in a bottle that famously failed to break on its first brush with the ship's stern. With this ritual, *HMS Dreadnought* was launched into the Solent, stirring up waves which would be felt around the world. Though Britain had intended to use Dreadnought to overawe potential rivals with her naval power, the revolutionary nature of its design immediately reduced Britain's 25-ship superiority in battleships to 1. She was broken up for scrap in 1923.

East Wind. Harbinger of unfavourable events. An east wind is referred to in Bleak House by Charles Dickens. The character Mr Jarndyce uses it several times. Sherlock Holmes mentions the east wind in *His Last Bow* (published in 1917 but set on the eve of the First World War) where clearly Arthur Conan Doyle expresses his own feelings:

"There's an east wind coming, Watson."

"I think not, Holmes. It is very warm."

"Good old Watson! You are the one fixed point in a changing age. There's an east wind coming all the same, such a wind as never blew on England yet. It will be cold and bitter, Watson, and a good many of us may wither before its blast. But it's God's own wind none the less, and a cleaner, better, stronger land will lie in the sunshine when the storm has cleared."

Emprise. An adventurous, daring, or chivalric enterprise.

Entari. Loose garment worn indoors.

Five jack. The old impressive 'large white fiver'—five pounds sterling banknote, equivalent to Sterling £600 in 2015.

Galata Bridge. Spans the Golden Horn in Istanbul. From the end of the 19th century in particular, the bridge has featured in Turkish literature, theatre, poetry and novels. The first recorded bridge over the Golden Horn in Istanbul was built during the reign of Justinian the Great in the 6th century, close to the area near the Theodosian Land Walls at the western end of the city. The fifth Galata bridge was built just a few meters away from the previous bridge, between Karaköy and Eminönü, and completed in December 1994.

Ghillie suit, also known as a yowie suit, or camo tent. Type of camouflage clothing designed to resemble heavy foliage, typically a net or cloth garment covered in loose strips of burlap, cloth or twine, sometimes made to look like leaves and twigs, and augmented with scraps of foliage from the area. Military snipers, hunters and nature photographers wear ghillie suits to blend into their surroundings. The suit gives the wearer's outline a three-dimensional breakup, rather than a linear one. When manufactured correctly, the suit will move in the wind in the same way as surrounding foliage.

Gieves. Founded in 1771 and now owned by Hong Kong conglomerate Trinity Ltd. Gieves business was originally based on catering for the needs of the British Army and the Royal Navy, and hence by association the British Royal family. In their various incarnations and premises they made uniforms for Admiral Lord Nelson and the Duke of Wellington. In 1974 Gieves Ltd acquired Hawkes and became Gieves & Hawkes., but still informally known just as 'Gieves' (pronounced 'Jeeves').

Grisette (or grizette). A French working-class woman from the late 17th century. The term remained in common use through the Belle Époque era. From gris, (French for grey), referring to the cheap grey fabric of the dresses these women originally wore.

Guinguettes. Popular drinking establishments in Parisian suburbs. Guinguettes also served as restaurants and, often, as dance venues. From guinguet, a sour white light local wine.

Harem. 'Forbidden place; sacrosanct, sanctum' for female members of the family. The term originated with the Near East. Harems are the portion of households occupied by wives and often sex slaves known as concubines.

Haroony. The author's partner Lesley Abdela is the granddaughter of the Victorian/Edwardian ship-builders Abdela & Mitchell on the Manchester Ship Canal and Stroud. The real *Haroony* was a 14 tonne craft launched in 1903, destined for Turkey or a Turkish domain. She was delivered by Isaac Abdela and Sophie Moss on their honeymoon via the Riviera, Italy and Greece, back to where the Abdelas had originated before the 1860s.

Ikbal. The harem member with whom the Sultan had slept at least once. These women need not necessarily have given a child to the Sultan but simply have taken his fancy.

Junior United Services Club. Founded 1815, disbanded in 1978. Located in Pall Mall, members were princes of the blood royal, commissioned officers of the Navy, Army, Marines, Royal Indian Forces, and Regular Militia, Lieutenants of Counties, sub-lieutenants in the Army and midshipmen in the Navy. 'No officer is eligible for admission to the club who is not on full, half or retired full-pay of the Navy, Army, Marines, or Royal Indian Forces; or who, if an officer of Militia, has not one year's embodied service or attended three regular trainings, certified by the commanding officer, adjutant, or paymaster of the regiment.' From Dickens's Dictionary of London, 1879, by Charles Dickens Jr.

Kadin. Among the women of the Imperial Harem, the Kadın was a woman who was not an official wife but had borne the Sultan a child, preferably a son.

KCMG. Order of St. Michael and St. George. The Star and Badge of the Order feature the cross of St George, the Order's motto, and a representation of the archangel St Michael holding in his right hand a flaming sword and trampling upon Satan. Unlike Sherlock, Mycroft Holmes had no hesitation in accepting a Knighthood albeit with a great sense of irony in this instance as he had intended to scupper Sherlock Holmes's mission.

Keffiyeh. Traditional Middle Eastern headdress fashioned from a square scarf, usually made of cotton.

Kiosk (from Turkish köşk). A small, separated garden pavilion open on some or all sides. Kiosks were common in Persia, the Indian subcontinent, and in the Ottoman Empire from the 13th century onward.

L'illusion des sosies. Now often called the Capgras delusion or Capgras syndrome. Disorder in which a person holds a delusion that a friend, spouse, parent, or other close family member (even pet) has been replaced by an identical-looking impostor.

Mackintosh, abbreviated as mac or mack, is a form of waterproof raincoat made out of rubberised fabric, first sold in 1824. It is named after its Scottish inventor Charles Macintosh, though many writers add a letter k (the spelling 'Mackintosh' is now widespread).

Mortuus. Deceased.

Ohne Hast, aber ohne Rast. Without haste, but without rest. Johann Wolfgang von Goethe.

Opera seria. Italian musical term for the noble and "serious" style of Italian opera predominant in Europe from the 1710s to c. 1770.

Politique de bascule. Used here to describe how a lesser power tries to trade off two or more Great Powers to gain an advantage. *Bascule* is a French term for seesaw and balance.

Puggried sun-hat. Broad brimmed felt hat with a muslin wrapped round it and trailing down the back.

Princes Islands: during the Byzantine period, princes and other royalty were exiled on the islands. Members of the Ottoman sultans' family were later exiled there too, giving the islands their present name. The islands were captured by the Ottoman fleet during the siege of Constantinople in 1453. During the nineteenth century, the islands became a popular resort for Istanbul's wealthier inhabitants.

Race-built ships. In 1570 with England threatened by Spain, Sir John Hawkins made important improvements in ship construction and rigging. They proved decisive against the Spanish Armada. The ships were 'race-built', longer and with fore- and aft-castle greatly reduced in size. They were described as having "the head of a cod and the tail of a mackerel".

Rahat loukoum. Turkish Delight. See 'Sherbet & Spice' in 'Publications'.

Raki. A traditional Turkish alcoholic drink produced from different fruits in differing regions, mainly grapes, figs and plums. In 1630, the famous Turkish traveller Evliya Çelebi listed the artisans of Istanbul in the first volume of his book on his voyages, recording the small wine shops and the kinds of wine they sold and also mentioned the taverns that sold raki, like raki wine, banana raki, mustard raki, linden raki, cinnomon raki, clove raki, pomegranate raki, aniseed raki.

Scatter-gun with S.S.G. Special Small Game. Archaic British designation for a size of buck shot. A potent, short range (40 yds extreme max.) hunting load for four-legged game.

Sherry Cobbler. The most popular drink in America around 1888, according to David Wondrich's *Imbibe!*, but also a hit elsewhere in the world. The key to any cobbler is crushed ice, sugar, and a heaping of fresh fruit such as strawberries for the garnish. The cobbler style of cocktails can be made with any base, not just sherry, for example brandy or whiskey. The Cobbler spawned a number of similar wine cobblers made with a variety of wines of the time which are now for the most part extinct.

Silks. Heavy silks such as kemha (brocade), kadife (velvet), çatma (brocaded velvet), seraser (a precious silk fabric woven with threads of gold and silver), diba (a silk brocade), satin, and silk lampas, lighter silks such as taffeta, canfes (fine taffeta), and vala (a gauze like fabric). By the late 19th Century the Ottoman Empire was producing only inferior quality silks. Imports from Europe were preferred.

Simpson's Grand Cigar Divan. After a modest start in 1828 as a smoking room and then a coffee house, Simpson's Restaurant achieved fame around 1850 for its traditional English food, particularly roast meats.

Snipers. This particularly frightening element in warfare advanced as rifles, cartridges and telescopic sights develop in later Victorian times. By World War 11 and through the Korean War, Vietnam, Lebanon, Iraq etc. military snipers honed their 'art', delivering a single deadly shot from up to 1½ miles (over 2.4 kilometres).

Spider phaeton. A carriage of American origin and made for gentlemen drivers, a very high carriage of light construction with a covered seat in front and a footman's seat behind.

Stambouline. A rather unattractive frock coat for formal occasions worn by Turkish officials. Copied from Victorian era European fashions.

Syenite. Coarse-grained intrusive igneous rock. Somewhat like granite but with the quartz either absent or present in relatively small amounts.

Telegrams of support. The Sultan showed Holmes and Watson a pile of telegrams supportive of his rule. In 1916, one of Tsar Nicholas's adulatory Ministers, Protopopoff, arranged for bogus telegrams to be dispatched in similar fashion to the German-born Empress, convincing her the Russian Army and peasantry were utterly loyal. Less than a year later the Romanov Dynasty fell.

Tigers. Either Holmes was being amusing or he did not know there are no tigers in Africa (except in the occasional zoo).

'The toad beneath the harrow.' A proverbial saying for a sufferer, dating back to the 13th Century. A harrow is a heavy frame with spikes dragged across a field by horses or a tractor to cultivate the soil. Clearly a toad beneath it would not survive very long.

Tophane. A neighbourhood in the Beyoğlu district of Istanbul, Turkey, taking its name from the Gun Foundry. It has a coastline with the Bosphorus. In the Ottoman era it was the city's oldest industrial zone.

Tussie-Mussie. From Queen Victoria's time when the small bouquets became a popular fashion accessory. Tussie-mussies include well-known floral symbolism from the language of flowers (e.g. Acacia blossom = hidden love), and therefore could be used to send a message to the recipient.

Verd-antique. Serpentinite breccia, popular since ancient times as a decorative facing stone. Dark, dull green, white-mottled (or white-veined) serpentine, mixed with calcite, dolomite, or magnesite, which takes a high polish.

Wardian case. Early type of terrarium, a sealed protective glass container for plants. Used in in the 19th century in protecting plants imported to Europe from overseas, most of which previously died from exposure on long sea journeys. Invented by Dr. Nathaniel Bagshaw Ward in about 1829.

Wideawake. A type of hat with a broad brim made of black or brown felt. Rembrandt wore a style of wideawake in his 1632 self-portrait. Also known as a Quaker hat.

Yataghan. Type of Ottoman knife or short sabre used from the mid-16th to late 19th centuries.

Lightning Source UK Ltd.
Milton Keynes UK
UKOW06f0941130715

255077UK00001B/5/P